W9-BXU-215

S > EAN

ISBN 978-0-593-19982-4

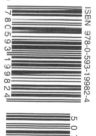

50799

WENDY WAX

A Ten Beach Road Christmas

PRAISE FOR THE NOVELS OF WENDY WAX

"[A] sparkling, deeply satisfying tale."
—Karen White, *New York Times* bestselling author

"Wax offers her trademark form of fiction, the beach read with substance." —*Booklist*

"Wax really knows how to make a cast of characters come alive . . . [She] infuses each chapter with enough drama, laughter, family angst, and friendship to keep readers greedily turning pages until the end."
—*RT Book Reviews*

"This season's perfect beach read!" —Single Titles

"A tribute to the transformative power of female friendship . . . Reading Wendy Wax is like discovering a witty, wise, and wonderful new friend."
—Claire Cook, *New York Times* bestselling author of *Must Love Dogs* and *Time Flies*

"If you're a sucker for plucky women who rise to the occasion, this is for you." —*USA Today*

continued . . .

Titles by Wendy Wax

Ten Beach Road Novels
(In Series Order)

TEN BEACH ROAD

OCEAN BEACH

CHRISTMAS AT THE BEACH
(eNovella)

THE HOUSE ON MERMAID POINT

SUNSHINE BEACH

ONE GOOD THING

A BELLA FLORA CHRISTMAS
(eNovella)

BEST BEACH EVER

Standalone Novels

MY EX-BEST FRIEND'S WEDDING

A WEEK AT THE LAKE

WHILE WE WERE WATCHING DOWNTON ABBEY

MAGNOLIA WEDNESDAYS

THE ACCIDENTAL BESTSELLER

SINGLE IN SUBURBIA

HOSTILE MAKEOVER

LEAVE IT TO CLEAVAGE

7 DAYS AND 7 NIGHTS

A TEN BEACH ROAD CHRISTMAS

WENDY WAX

BERKLEY
New York

BERKLEY
An imprint of Penguin Random House LLC
penguinrandomhouse.com

Copyright © 2017 by Wendy Wax
Christmas at the Beach copyright © 2014 by Wendy Wax
A Bella Flora Christmas copyright © 2017 by Wendy Wax
Excerpt from *Best Beach Ever* copyright © 2017 by Wendy Wax
Penguin Random House supports copyright. Copyright fuels creativity, encourages
diverse voices, promotes free speech, and creates a vibrant culture. Thank you for buying
an authorized edition of this book and for complying with copyright laws by not
reproducing, scanning, or distributing any part of it in any form without permission.
You are supporting writers and allowing Penguin Random House to continue to
publish books for every reader.

BERKLEY and the BERKLEY & B colophon
are registered trademarks of Penguin Random House LLC.

ISBN: 9780593199824

Berkley mass-market edition / November 2017
Berkley mass-market edition / October 2020

Printed in the United States of America
1   3   5   7   9   10   8   6   4   2

Cover art: Christmas berry wreath © Maria Dryfhout; Sand dune © Cheryl Casey
Cover design by Alana Colucci

This is a work of fiction. Names, characters, places, and incidents either are the product
of the author's imagination or are used fictitiously, and any resemblance to actual persons,
living or dead, business establishments, events, or locales is entirely coincidental.

If you purchased this book without a cover, you should be aware that this book is stolen
property. It was reported as "unsold and destroyed" to the publisher, and neither the author
nor the publisher has received any payment for this "stripped book."

Dear Reader,

Some authors know exactly where a story is headed before they sit down to write the first paragraph.

I am not one of those authors.

When I first introduced Madeline Singer, Avery Lawford, and Nicole Grant in *Ten Beach Road*, they were strangers and Ponzi scheme victims who woke up one day to discover that all they had left was shared ownership of Bella Flora, a crumbling 1920s Mediterranean style beachfront mansion. In that first (and I thought only) novel, they spend a long sweat-soaked summer bringing Bella Flora back to life. It does the same for them.

At the time, I had no idea *Ten Beach Road* would be the first of a series that now includes six novels and the two holiday novellas in this book. Did I mention I'm not a planner?

Because novellas (a fancier word for short story) are, well, shorter, *Christmas at Ten Beach Road* and *A Bella Flora Christmas* were originally published only in digital form, each at the time it was written.

Over the years, I've heard from many *Ten Beach Road* fans who wanted to read the holiday novellas in print. So I am incredibly happy to share with you this print edition of

A Ten Beach Road Christmas, which contains both holiday novellas in chronological order. You can read these novellas on their own. You are also free to read the series in any order you choose. (Each book stands on its own.) There are also notes on the title page of each novella indicating which Ten Beach Road novels it falls between. So whether you're a long-time Ten Beach Road fan catching up on a missed holiday novella (thanks!), or a brand-new-to-me reader (yay!), I'm so glad you're choosing to read *A Ten Beach Road Christmas*. I truly hope you enjoy spending time with Maddie, Avery, Nikki, and crew as much as I do.

Wishing you all the very best,
Wendy

PS: For more information on me and my novels, please visit my website, authorwendywax.com, where you can read descriptions and excerpts of all my novels, download book club kits and discussion questions, or send me an email. I love to hear from readers!

Contents

CHRISTMAS AT THE BEACH

This story takes place between the
novels *Ocean Beach* and
The House on Mermaid Point.

Chapter One

Having your own personal pack of paparazzi gives you sympathy for hunted animals and is nowhere near as exciting as people think. It wouldn't be quite so bad if they kept regular business hours—you know, showed up around nine and clocked out at five. But celebrity stalking is a twenty-four seven occupation with no time off for good—or bad—behavior. Because if they don't get pictures that make you look nasty, stupid, or even less attractive without makeup than the average tabloid reader, they don't eat.

Of course, it's a lot easier to become a celebrity today than it used to be. You can be famous now for the size of your boobs and butt, a five-minute cameo on a reality TV show, doing a below-average tango on *Dancing with the Stars*, or dating and/or marrying someone who's done any of the above. The celebrity bar has dropped so low that if it were being set for a game of Limbo, that bar would be ankle-height.

You can even become a celebrity by accident. I happen to know this because that's what happened to me.

My name is Kyra Singer, and I became famous for falling in love with a movie star named Daniel Deranian while I was working as a production assistant on my first feature film, believing him when he said he loved me, and then getting pregnant with his child.

I might regret this more if Dustin, who just turned one last month, weren't so incredible. And if Daniel's movie-star wife, Tonja Kay, were a normal human being whose head doesn't do a 360 when she gets pissed.

If Dustin is the best thing in all of this, and he is, the worst is the extra burden it put on my mother, who was handling a lot already when I got booted off the set by the head-spinning Tonja Kay and then sliced and diced in the tabloids.

Unlike a lot of other ankle-height celebrities, I'd way rather be behind the camera than in front of it. But today, which is Christmas Eve day, when I get out to the curb at the Tampa International Airport with my son, his car seat, our suitcase, and my film gear, a bunch of paparazzi are waiting at the curb. My mother and her minivan are not.

I'm careful not to make eye contact with any of them while I try to figure out what to do. I'm considering turning around and going back inside to regroup, when a text dings in. It's from my missing mother. It reads *Sri. My fats in fyre.*

I read it twice, but it doesn't get any clearer. My mother, Madeline, is fifty-one, and she's impressive as hell in a lot of respects, but I think she communicated way better before her phone got so smart. Her next text reads *Sree. Mint tries flit.*

IMHO, most people over forty don't have control of their thumbs and shouldn't be allowed to text.

"Kyra, over here!" The accent is British and I recognize the voice. Every once in a while you're forced to realize that there are real people behind the cameras. People who barge into your life uninvited and then become strangely familiar.

I look up and see Nigel Bracken at the front of the pack. As always I try to shield Dustin as best I can, but he's one now and not a baby that I can hold in any position I want. Plus he's a veritable clone of his movie-star father, with the same golden-skinned face, dark brown eyes, and curly hair. The paparazzi can't get enough of him. A couple of weeks ago a crazed Daniel Deranian fan stole one of Dustin's dirty diapers out of the trash and tried to sell it on eBay. That's how weird it gets sometimes.

"Over here, Kyra!" another one of the paps shouts. His name's Bill and he has bad teeth and a potato shaped nose. They are their own League of Nations—American, British, French, and lots of Heinz 57s. They're tall and skinny, short and round, and everything in between. Some of them are good-looking enough to walk the red carpet. Others, like Bill, have faces only a mother could love. You rarely see women doing this. I like to think it's because women are too smart and sympathetic to view stalking celebrities as gainful employment, but it could just be that, like the movie business, it's a good old boys' club that women have to work twice as hard and be twice as talented to break into.

"Just give us a couple shots and we're out of here!" Nigel shouts.

This is a lie. One clean shot will madden them like bees whose hive has been swatted. When I don't respond, they surge closer.

An airport security guard passes by and warns them to keep out of the traffic lanes.

The transportation line is downstairs and so are the car rental desks. What I really need to do is call my mother and find out why she's not here, but I don't want to do this on-camera. Most of these guys can read lips better than an NFL coach with a pair of binoculars trying to decipher the other team's plays.

"Come on, Kyra, luv! It's practically Christmas! Give us a smile!" I'm not sure who died and elected Nigel spokesman, but at least they're not all yelling at once.

Dustin's arm loops up around my neck, and he lifts his head from my shoulder. "Krimas!" he says. The camera drives whir and the digital flashes explode.

I feel the pack moving in, and I fall back a step, not wanting to be surrounded. I turn and move quickly—I prefer not to think of it as running—into the terminal. I head for the only place I might be safe: the ladies' room.

In a locked stall I check the floor on either side to make sure there are no size-twelve shoes. I drop our suitcase and my camera bag on the floor, stand the folded stroller in a corner, and perch gingerly on the edge of the toilet seat with Dustin in my lap. I could text my mother—she reads texts better than she sends them—but then she might text me back and if I can't read it it will be another big waste of time. I hit speed dial for her number.

"Mom?" I keep my voice down when the phone is answered just in case. And because it's always kind of gross when you hear someone making a phone call from the toilet regardless of what they are or aren't doing there.

"Oh, Kyra, thank goodness." My mother sounds agitated and out of breath. "I'm so sorry, sweetie. I had a flat tire on the Bayway and I'm still waiting for AAA." I can picture the beige-gold minivan on the side of the causeway that leads from Pass-a-Grille Beach, through Tierra Verde, to the interstate, while Cadillacs and old Chryslers putter past. The population of St. Petersburg and its environs is largely elderly. The joke goes if you leave a glass of water sitting out someone will put his or her teeth in it. My mom hasn't even made it off the beach. Even if she got the tire fixed in the next five minutes, which is unlikely, she wouldn't be here for another thirty-five minutes after that.

"Don't worry about it. I'll rent a car and meet you at Bella Flora."

"Are you sure?" My mother has witnessed the paparazzi up close and personal from the day they first found me while we were desperately trying to restore Bella Flora, which is a really cool Mediterranean Revival–style home that was built in the 1920s and was all my mother and the equally unfortunate Avery Lawford and Nicole Grant had left after they lost everything to Malcolm Dyer's Ponzi scheme. That's where I'm headed right now.

"Absolutely. Who's at the house?"

"Avery, Deirdre, and Nicole are there. Chase and his sons are joining us tomorrow morning to open presents. Your dad and Andrew are driving down from Atlanta today."

"Okay. I'm going to pick up a car. I'll take the Bayway from 275 so I can stop and help if you're still there."

"Be careful. I don't want them chasing after you and Dustin."

I know from the way she says this that she's thinking

about what happened to Princess Diana. But I'm not a princess, and the Howard Frankland Bridge to St. Pete is not a Paris tunnel. Still, it will be better if I can just disappear. I don't want to lead the paparazzi to Bella Flora, even though I'm sure they all already know that Dustin and I are headed to Ten Beach Road.

"We'll be fine," I say because we've had this conversation before. Or at least we will be, once I put on my disguise.

The car rental agent looks at my driver's license and then up at my face. Or rather what can be seen of my face, namely my eyes. "Eees there a problem?" I ask in what I would like to believe is a decent Middle Eastern accent.

"I'm, ah, afraid I need to ask you to uncover your face for just a moment, Ms. . . . Singer." It's unfortunate that my disguise, politically incorrect as it might be, comes with a veil but not a fake ID. I've worn the burqa before because it's easy to slip on over whatever I'm wearing. Unlike some of my other disguises, it covers almost all of me. From the back, which is all anyone including a photographer walking by right now can see, the only thing it gives away is my height. My son has Armenian blood, courtesy of his father, and can pass for vaguely Middle Eastern. I'm a hundred percent white bread, and while I'm not a dog or anything, nothing about me is the least bit exotic.

When we were working on the house in South Beach and shooting the first season of *Do Over*, Daniel used to come in disguise to see Dustin. Honestly, he looks just as good in a miniskirt and heels or doddering on a cane as he does on the big screen. But then he was in Miami shooting a film and had a whole makeup and special effects department at his disposal.

I look to both sides and behind me before I undo my veil from the headscarf and hold it slightly away from my face so the agent can compare it to my driver's license photo, which, let's face it, is virtually unrecognizable and completely unflattering.

He looks up and down a few times just to be sure, taking in my gray eyes and pale skin. He's clearly registered that I'm not Middle Eastern and that I'm traveling without a male family member. I hope he doesn't recognize my name or my child. Any one of the paparazzi would pay good money for this information. I hide a smile at the idea of them chasing after every woman in the airport wearing a burqa, but the sooner I get us out of here and on the road, the better.

"What size car would you like?"

What I really want is something built like a tank and with darkened windows, so that if I mow down a few photographers no one will see the satisfaction on my face, but I just ask for a midsize, which I understand is what used to be called compact. The weather is gorgeous—all pale blue sky and puffy clouds and what feels like a perfect seventy degrees. It's convertible weather—but it wouldn't do to whip by the waiting paparazzi with my veil flying in the breeze. Would it?

Once I'm safely out of the airport grounds and lost in traffic, I unzip the burqa, drop the veil in the back seat next to Dustin, then open the windows so I can feel the air on my face. When I hit the bridge the air takes on a salty tinge and I can see the Courtney Campbell Causeway, which leads to Clearwater, on my right. The Gandy Bridge stretches north and south on my left. I spent a long, sweat-soaked summer while I was pregnant with Dustin working on and shooting the renovation of Bella Flora, so the Tampa Bay area, and especially St. Pete Beach, feels almost as much like home as Atlanta. At the time I was posting snarky comments and video of the renovation online while I waited for Daniel to come whisk me away on his white horse. He did

show up, but only to offer me a position as his mistress—
a position I declined. My video and the audience my
posts drew led to our Lifetime TV series, *Do Over*.
Which is almost as much about fixing our lives as it is
about fixing the houses the network has started throwing at us.

Dustin is asleep by the time I get off the bridge and
onto 275 heading south. His long dark lashes cast mini-
shadows on his golden skin. I look for my mom's van
when I turn onto the Pinellas Bayway, but it's nowhere
to be seen, so I assume she'll be waiting at Bella Flora.
The waterfront condos and a golf course whip by. In
minutes I'm over the final bridge and stopped at a red
light in front of the Don CeSar Hotel—a huge pink and
white castle-like structure built in the same Mediterranean Revival style as Bella Flora. I turn left onto Gulf
Boulevard and the road narrows as I enter the historic
district of Pass-a-Grille, which occupies the southernmost tip of St. Pete Beach.

Cutting over to Gulf Way, I get my first full-on
glimpse of the Gulf of Mexico and the wide white-sand
beach that bounds it. I draw in another breath of salt-
tinged air and drive slowly to drink it all in. Little
mom-and-pop hotels slide by on my left. It's all beach

and dunes and boardwalks over them on my right. The blocks are short and the avenues, which stretch between the gulf and the bay, are barely longer.

The streetlights are garland-wrapped, with great big red bows tied at the top. There are lots of blow-up Santas and palm-tree trunks wrapped in Christmas lights. I pass the Paradise Grille, the beach trolley stop, and the Hurricane Restaurant, which has been around forever despite a name that seems to be just asking for trouble.

Eighth Avenue is Pass-a-Grille's "main street," with its shops, restaurants, and galleries, and I see that someone has strung lights across it. I grew up in Atlanta, which isn't exactly the frozen tundra, but it's still weird to see people walking around in shorts and T-shirts on December 24. The soundtrack, courtesy of Mother Nature, is all palm fronds stirring in the breeze and waves washing gently onto the sand. Seagulls caw loudly as they zigzag through the sky.

At the very southernmost tip, where the gulf and bay meet, I come to Ten Beach Road. In the afternoon sun, Bella Flora looks fresh out of the bakery box. Its pale pink walls and acres of windows are trimmed in white icing and accented by bell towers and wrought-iron balconies. The whole confection is topped by a multi-angled barrel-tile roof.

Avery Lawford's bright blue Mini Cooper and Nicole Grant's classic green Jaguar are already parked in the bricked drive. My mother's minivan, tires intact, is pulled in behind them. I've never seen cars that so perfectly personify their owners.

"Gee-ma." Dustin has his nose pressed against the car window. He's madly in love with his grandmother and knows her van when he sees it.

"That's right. Gee-ma is here. And Grandpa and Doo will be here tonight." It's an eight-hour drive down, and my dad and brother, Andrew, are bound to already be on the road.

The garden is lush even in the winter and beautifully maintained. Our Realtor's wife and her gardening club of electric-saw-toting octogenarians are the ones who brought the original 1920s garden back from decades of neglect. The leaping-dolphin fountain sprays a welcome gush of water.

I pull in next to the low cement wall that fronts the garden and try not to notice the sold sign that dangles over it. I was a scared, pregnant kid running to her mother the first time I came here. Today I have a child of my own, who I love more than anything, and a chance at building a television career. My life hasn't turned out remotely like I planned, but almost everything good that's happened began right here. This is the first and last Christmas we'll ever celebrate at Ten Beach Road.

Chapter Two

There's no sign of the paparazzi—I hope they're still camped out at the airport waiting for me to come back out—but I leave the burqa on and drape the veil over one arm just in case I need it to slip out of the house later. I do have a few other disguises packed away, but if no one's figured out this one yet, I might be able to pass as a Middle Eastern nanny or distant family member. Shrugging into my backpack, I scoop Dustin out of his car seat and settle him on my hip so that I can carry in a bag of camera gear.

My son's huge brown eyes crane upward to take in the impressive house that was little more than a ruin the first time I saw it. "Bella Flora," I say carefully and watch him consider the words. "You were in my tummy the first time you came here."

"Buhfora," he says solemnly, trying it on for size. Dustin started talking really early, but sometimes you have to focus to figure out what he's saying. When his smile flashes in satisfaction he looks just like Daniel, but there's a gentle happiness at the center of Dustin that I envy sometimes. And an occasional gravity that makes me think he understands a lot more than a one-year-old possibly could.

The kitchen door is unlocked and I wrangle it open, drop the gear on the floor, and manage to close the door with my foot. My mother is there puttering and organizing, which is not too surprising. If you look in the dictionary under the word *mother*, you'll probably find a picture of mine. Hearing us, she turns and smiles. Dustin gives a little squeal of happiness. I know the feeling.

I hope I look like my mother does when I'm in my fifties. She complains about gravitational pull and all that, but she looks like a mother should, soft and warm and inviting and maybe just a little faded around the edges. It's only in the last year and a half that I found out there's a steel rod that runs right through her.

"There you are!" She hugs us both and takes Dustin out of my arms. I know my mother loves me, but ever since I gave birth I'm definitely coming in second. "Hello, little man," she coos. "Would you like some juice?"

Dustin's smile gets bigger. "Duce!"

"Sorry I didn't get there," she says. "Did you have any trouble getting a car?"

"No. Eet was not too hard." I hold the veil up just beneath my eyes and bat my lashes at her. "Although I have been in theese country many years I am still working on my Eengleesh."

"God, I hate that you have to disguise yourself just to be left in peace. Daniel Dcranian has a lot to answer for."

I shrug. As much as I'd like to blame everything on Daniel, I made my choices and I need to make the best of them. I'm learning how to navigate the circus, but that doesn't mean I like it. It's kind of like having a permanent skin condition. You don't have to hide inside all the time. You can go out in the world with it, but you're always aware of it. And it colors everything. Someday I probably won't be tabloid-worthy, but I'll always be the production assistant who got kicked off her very first feature film for having Daniel Deranian's baby.

"Where is everybody?" I ask.

"Avery and Deirdre are in the family room discussing the right spot for the Christmas tree. It could take a while."

Avery's a trained architect and completely competent in construction because she grew up on her father's construction sites; there would be no *Do Over* without her. She's small and curvy with blond hair and blue eyes, which annoys the hell out of her and makes her all about trying to command respect. Her mother, Deirdre, left for a long stretch of Avery's life to become an interior designer to the stars in Hollywood. My mother actually gave Deirdre mothering lessons while we were in South Beach, but Deirdre tends to pick and choose the parts that appeal to her.

"Nicole went out for a run," my mother continues. "When she gets back we're going to decorate the tree. Then we'll have our traditional drinks out around the pool at sunset."

"Sounds great. Where should I put our stuff?" I'm already halfway out the door toward the pool house when she says, "You and Dustin will bunk with me. I already set up the portable crib."

I turn. "But Dad's going to be here."

My mother shrugs and hands Dustin the juice cup. "Oh, I figured he and Andrew would be more comfortable out in the pool house." She doesn't exactly meet my eyes when she says this.

This is weird. Except for the time my dad spent on the couch with the remote glued to his hand after he lost his job and all our money—and the time they were apart while she helped renovate Bella Flora and The Millicent down in Miami—my dad and mom have always slept together. I mean, I don't know what they do in bed—that would be TMI—but they've always shared one. One of my earliest memories is racing into their bedroom and jumping between them on weekend mornings when I was little.

"That way I can help with Dustin if he wakes up at night. And Avery and Nicole won't have to share a bathroom with your dad. Or vice versa."

"Okay." I guess after you've been married for more than a quarter of a century, sleeping apart isn't exactly the end of the world. With a quick look outside to make sure nobody—especially nobody with a camera—is hanging around, I head back to the rental car to get the rest of our stuff, which I carry up to my mom's room at the front of the house. Avery, Mom, and Nicole, who are the primary owners along with Chase Hardin, the hunky contractor who headed up the renovation and is now Avery's main squeeze, each have a room. Deirdre, who somehow nabbed the master bedroom the day she arrived uninvited and still hasn't given it up, has a huge suite all to herself.

I haul our stuff up the front stairs and I can't help remembering the first time I saw them. The wood balustrade was scarred and damaged, the plaster walls were gouged and stained, and a Frankenstein monster labeled Malcolm Dyer was hanging over the banister in effigy. Of course, nobody knew then that Malcolm Dyer was Nicole's brother. If my brother ever stole everything from me, I'd do more than help put him in jail. I'd make sure he was sleeping with the fishes or having birds peck out his eyeballs or some other fitting cinematic retribution.

I lean out the open bedroom window and look down the beach. Sunshine glints off the gulf and a stream of people walk near the water's edge. Boats bob out in the distance and a few people are fishing off the pier. Down near the Don CeSar, someone's parasailing, just dangling in the harness. It looks like a summer day out there, but if he's smart, he's wearing a wet suit.

By the time I get down to the salon that stretches across the back of the house, my mom has Dustin playing with a box of wood blocks and is mediating the tree placement. Avery and Deirdre stop arguing long enough to give me hugs. Avery's practically a mirror image of her mother, though we're all really careful not to point this out. They both have chests that are too big for the rest of them, but Avery, whose first network turned her into the Vanna White of the DIY set, tries to hide hers, while Deirdre is all about tasteful showcasing.

"Every time I disagree with her she rubs her arm like it still hurts," Avery complains as she tightens the tree stand.

"I never said it hurt," Deirdre replies, standing back to eye the tree, which as far as I'm concerned is in the perfect spot in the exact middle of the run of floor-to-ceiling windows. The view of the pool and the pass, where the bay and the gulf meet, is spectacular from here.

"No, but you're forever reminding me that you took a bullet for me," Avery says.

"I am not." Deirdre turns to Mom and me. "Can I help it if it aches a little bit now and then?"

"Like when I don't immediately do whatever she wants."

"You never do what I want." Deirdre rubs her arm where the bullet entered when she threw herself in front of Avery just as the gun went off down in South Beach. I hold on to the box I brought down with me.

Nicole Grant comes in through the French doors that open onto the loggia. She's tall and willowy with deep red hair and great skin. She always runs in designer running clothes and she looks good even when she's sweating. Her eyes are a sharp green that can cut right through you and any bullshit you might be slinging. I'm not sure how old she is—somewhere between forty and fifty, but I don't know which end. She used to be a famous dating guru and A-list matchmaker until her brother stole everything she had in his three-hundred-million-dollar Ponzi scheme and the press got hold of the fact that they're related. I guess her bullshit-ometer works better on strangers than family. Though come to think of it, it didn't work all that well on Parker Amherst IV, the alleged matchmaking client in Miami who was looking for revenge on her brother and not, as Nikki thought, a wife. It was his bullet that landed in Deirdre's arm. And ended Max Golden's life.

Crap. Every time I think about Max my eyes get all wet. He might have been ninety but he had so much life left in him. And he did take the bullet that was intended for Dustin.

I open the box I brought down with me and pull out the menorah and candles I bought in Max's honor. The menorah has candle holders shaped like comedy masks because Max and his wife Millie were once the George Burns and Gracie Allen of Miami Beach. I set it on the mantel. Just looking at it makes me smile.

"Are you thinking about converting?" Nicole asks when she notices the menorah and sees me opening the box of candles.

"No. I just thought we might light the candles tonight after the sun goes down," I say.

"I'm pretty sure Hanukkah's already over, sweetie. It's not always at Christmas." My mom says this gently like she does most things. All of us were attached to Max and The Millicent, his cool nautical Art Deco home that we renovated for the first full season of *Do Over.* I wonder if they miss him as much as I do.

"Yeah. I know. But I want Dustin to know who Max

was and how much Max cared about him." Max had already been teaching Dustin about comedy and timing. "And, I don't know, I just thought it would be a cool thing to do."

"I'm in as long as I don't have to eat potato pancakes," Nikki says. "I'm still trying to get rid of the pounds I put on at the Giraldis' Thanksgiving. I'm not used to celebrating all these food holidays." Joe Giraldi's the FBI agent who tried to use her to help track down her brother. How twisted is that? He's completely hot for an older guy and she's been living in Miami with him since we finished renovating The Millicent. They've got something going on; I just don't know exactly what.

"If I spend another holiday with the Giraldis, I'm going to end up on *The Biggest Loser*."

"How was it?" my mom asks.

"It was good," Nikki says. "If you like eating massive amounts of food and fending off questions about your intentions. As if I'm going to somehow hurt Joe when he's the one who carries a gun and tries to catch bad guys." Her cheeks are all pink, and I don't think it's from running.

"Are we set?" My mother looks at the tree and then turns her steely-eyed mom gaze on Avery and Deirdre.

They nod without looking at each other. "Good." She hands out packages of tinsel and boxes of ornaments that I recognize from home. There are candy canes and long strings of popcorn just like we used to make when I was little. The box she hands me has the ornaments I made in kindergarten and elementary school.

"Come here, Dustin." She smiles and extends a box out toward my son. "These are yours." His eyes light up and I watch her help him put them on the lowest branches; there's a fire truck and a snowman and a palm tree that says Pass-a-Grille on it. My heart does a weird kind of thump when I realize that in a few years he'll be bringing ornaments home from school. My mom brings out a pitcher of eggnog and some glasses and Dustin's refilled sippy cup of juice. Somebody, I think it's Nicole, puts on some holiday music. It's way too warm for a fire in the fireplace, but we go to town on the tree. After a few cups of the eggnog, even Avery and Deirdre are harmonizing to the Christmas carols.

I can practically feel Bella Flora wrapping her arms around us, gathering us close, and telling us how much she's going to miss us.

Chapter Three

"Come on," my mom says after I've climbed the ladder and helped Dustin put the star at the very top of the tree. "It's almost sunset. I hope you've all got a good thing in mind." In the direst days of Bella Flora's desperate renovation, Mom made everyone come up with one good thing that had happened that day. Believe me, sometimes it wasn't easy.

The sun is weakening and everyone puts on jackets and sweaters and we head outside carrying our drinks and snacks. There's a bowl of Avery's Cheez Doodles; a plate of the little stuffed hot dogs and Bagel Bites that I like; some animal crackers for Dustin. Deirdre's carrying a tray with caviar, crackers, and the fancy stuff that goes on them. She's not a big believer in roughing it.

"Seriously?" Avery rolls her eyes at her mother. If a snack doesn't turn her fingers orange, Avery's not interested.

Nicole brings out a pitcher of frozen margaritas, which is not exactly the perfect chaser to eggnog. "Hey, I know it's Christmas, but we *are* at the beach." No one argues with this. We've done a ton of sunsets right here with Bella Flora hunkered down protectively around us and most of them have been fueled by a frozen drink of some kind.

We settle in our chairs—the really nice wrought-iron ones that replaced the original folding beach chairs my mom bought at a yard sale—and set the food and drink on the little tables that go with them. Dustin plops down in the sandbox that Avery built for him and starts digging. It's on the loggia, which means he can't get past us to the pool. He likes to dig on the beach the best, but the temperature's dropping with the sun and I'm still keeping an eye out for Nigel and the other photographers. If I'm lucky, they spotted a real celebrity or two at the airport and followed them.

I pull out my video camera and nobody complains. It was my video that led to our television show on Lifetime. I get a wide shot of the sun hanging in the sky and do a slow tilt and pan across all four of their faces.

"Okay. I'll go first to kind of prime the pump," Mom says. "My good thing is that my family and my friends"—she looks at every one of us—"will all be here to celebrate the holiday in my favorite place on earth."

"I'm glad to be alive." Deirdre rubs her arm and I zoom in on a loose two-shot so that Avery's eye roll is obvious. "And here. And spending Christmas Eve with the people I care most about, too." Avery's eyes don't roll this time. In fact, they look decidedly damp. Or maybe it's just the sun's reflection.

"Well, I think having a buyer for Bella Flora is a good thing, right?" Nikki says. "I mean, we all need the money. And we never intended to keep her." Her whole statement is a question, which is not at all like Nicole. She's right, though, there was a time when everyone assumed that bringing Bella Flora back after so many years of neglect was all about selling her so that we could get our lives back. But you can't work on a house like this with your own hands and still think of it as just brick and mortar.

"She's eighty-five years old. Nothing that goes wrong with her is inexpensive," Deirdre says.

"I know the feeling," Nicole says.

Deirdre, who's the oldest of all of us, and probably the best maintained, says, "She needs to belong to someone who can not only enjoy her but afford to maintain her."

That would not be us. Once the money's split among my mom, Avery, Nicole, and Chase—who paid out-of-pocket for the hard costs of renovation in exchange for a piece of the profits—no one's going to be left with all that much. And the future of our remodeling-series-turned-reality-show is a lot less certain than any of us would like.

"Well, I'd feel a lot better about it if we knew who the buyer was," Avery says. "How do we know what their intentions are?"

"Oh, my God, you sound like Joe's mother," Nicole says. "This is the first serious buyer we've had. It doesn't matter what his or her intentions are. Besides, who's going to pay almost three million dollars for a house and then tear it down?"

"A rich stupid person," Avery says. "Having money doesn't give you taste. Or make you smart."

This is true. Sometimes having a ton of money can make you incredibly nasty. Take Tonja Kay, for instance. I get that she's pissed off at how Daniel screws around. I mean, I wasn't the first or last—I just happen to be the only one who's given him a son so far. I might even feel sorry for her if she didn't spend her free time adopting children and harassing anyone Daniel is attracted to.

"Well, holding on to money in today's economy indicates a certain level of intelligence," Nicole points out.

It's hard to argue with this, so we just sip our drinks. Avery has a red margarita stain around her mouth, and her fingers are Cheez Doodle orange. Deirdre looks like she's ready for her photo shoot, but then I guess you eat caviar in such small doses there isn't much left to smear around.

My mother looks at me and I know it's my turn. I settle the video camera in my lap while I try to come up with a good thing other than Dustin. And the fact that although Daniel can't be trusted or counted on emotionally, he's extremely generous. Which is why I don't have to work multiple jobs or lean too heavily on my parents to take care of our son.

"*Do Over*'s a good thing, right?" my mother prompts.

They all look at me, since I'm the only one who's seen the edited first season, which is set to air this spring.

"Yeah." I'm not really ready to talk about this, but it doesn't look like I'm going to be given a choice.

"That didn't sound so good," Avery says. "What's the problem?"

I try not to fidget in my seat. "Well, they really played up Max's missing son. And Daniel's visits to see Dustin. And Parker Amherst's spectacular, um, meltdown. And, of course, our, um, personal issues." I stop talking. Everyone looks a little sick to their stomachs at the reminder that anyone who chooses to tune in—and we need there to be a ton of them—is going to know all kinds of things about us that we don't want them to. "Troy kept Lisa Hogan happy." I almost gag on the nasty network head's name. "But he did try to protect us. In his way." My voice peters out. "Can my good thing be that we could have looked worse?"

There's an uncomfortable beat of silence.

"I'm not the good-enough police," Mom says, just like she always does. But I can see how worried they look.

"Your turn," Mom says to Avery.

Avery squirms in her seat. I don't know if it's because

she hates admitting to anything good in front of Deirdre or something's going on between her and Chase; Avery and Chase remind me of the whole two dogs, one bone thing.

"Well, I do like working for my dad's company. With Chase and his father." She kind of mumbles this last part. "And with Deirdre." This last is so quiet I almost miss it. "There's a continuity to it that feels . . . good." Her chin juts out and she pops a Cheez Doodle in her mouth then chews it defiantly.

Deirdre looks like somebody handed her a million dollars. Which maybe someone has. I mean I can't imagine leaving Dustin, not even with my mother, to go off and have my own life. Taking that bullet was such a motherly thing to do. Plus Deirdre's been groveling for a while now. I'm no expert, but it seems to be working.

The sun is pretty low now, hanging just above the horizon. Sunsets are different in the winter—less "look at me" and more "done for the day, catch you tomorrow." But it's still beautiful.

We sit in silence as the sky turns a pale gray. The shadows on Bella Flora's pink plaster walls deepen as the sky fades to black.

"Time to light the candles," I say as I lift Dustin out

of the sandbox and kind of fold him over one arm so I can brush the sand off his behind. "We're going to celebrate Hanukkah for Max."

"Gax!" I don't know what my son remembers, but the name still means something to him.

Inside I put a candle in each of the eight holders then light the one that's called the shamas. *Sorry, Max,* I think, as I read the English transliteration of the Hebrew prayer phonetically—and badly, I'm sure—while I light each candle, moving from right to left just like in the video I watched on YouTube. The translation, which I also read aloud, thanks God, who "commands us to kindle the Hanukkah lights."

We all watch the flames flicker. Even with the comedy mask–shaped holders, the menorah appears stark compared to the frolic of color and shape on the Christmas tree. But none of us can look away. "I have a present for you from Max," I say to my son. I hand him the blue-and-white-wrapped box and help him unwrap the framed photo of him and Max "discussing" comedic timing that I shot last summer in Miami. He stares down at Max Golden's weathered face, with its oversize but distinguished nose and intelligent brown eyes. His caterpillar eyebrows are the same white as his close-cropped hair and are raised so high they almost reach it. The smile is Max's dazzling megawatter, and the twinkle in his eyes is unmistakable. An unlit cigar is clenched between two gnarled fingers.

"Gax!" Dustin pulls the photo up against his chest like he's never going to let it go. I plan to make sure he never does.

Chapter Four

I've got Dustin bathed and tucked into the portable crib when the doorbell rings. I'm thinking it's Dad and Andrew until I hear the churning of gears and what sounds like a revving truck engine outside. Which is pretty strange given that it's eight o'clock on Christmas Eve and even UPS and FedEx are probably finished delivering by now.

"What's going on?" Everyone's huddled in the foyer. The front door is open and a man stands on the front mat.

"I have a delivery. For Dustin Deranian." He looks up from the paperwork. "I need him to sign for it."

"He's already gone night night," I say. "I'm his

mother." I scrawl my signature and scan the garden behind him. When I'm sure there are no paparazzi hiding in the bushes or behind our cars, we follow him outside to where a huge flatbed truck idles in the street. There's a house on it—one of those big wooden playhouses that kids can go inside. Only it's about ten times bigger than any I've ever seen and it looks exactly like Bella Flora. I mean, on the outside anyway, it's an exact replica. It's huge; all of us could probably stand up inside it.

"Where do you want it?"

I have no idea. The replica is strangely perfect and feels oddly personal—kind of like receiving an anatomically correct copy of yourself completely out of the blue—and part of me wants to refuse it. But a second delivery guy is already attaching the hook to the crane so that it can be off-loaded. It has the biggest red bow I've ever seen tied around it.

"Listen, lady, I'd like to get home in time to suit up and make an appearance before my kids go to bed." He has a huge beer belly and I'm sure he makes a convincing Santa. Except for the big "Mom" tattoo on his neck.

He hands me an envelope that has Dustin's name scrawled across the front in Daniel's handwriting. Not that anyone else could—or would—have sent anything this extravagant. Didn't I tell him we'd sold Bella Flora?

"Where do you want it?"

I still have no idea and look at the others helplessly.

"Maybe we can fit it around the pool as an additional guesthouse," Avery says. "It looks like it could sleep at least four."

"If we'd had it before, we could have bumped up the asking price," Deirdre adds.

"Do you think we can get it out back in the dark?" my mom asks.

We're still huddled and trying to figure it out when the first flashbulb goes off. *Shit.* I pull the hood up over my head and zip up my sweatshirt, but it doesn't cover anywhere near as much as the burqa. The house is still dangling as the paparazzi start begging for shots and shouting their stupid questions.

"Can you turn this way just a bit, Kyra, luv?" Nigel calls out. "Is it from Dustin's da? Did Daniel send it?"

I hate how they use everyone's first names as if they're friends who just happen to loiter outside and take unwanted pictures. So much for time off to observe the birth of Christ.

"It might fit on that side of the garden," Nicole says.

"No, not anywhere near those birds of paradise or the triple hibiscus. Renée Franklin and her garden ladies will never forgive us."

"We can't put it anywhere out front without blocking access of some kind," Nikki says.

"And anywhere near the center of the garden is going to put the fountain at risk," Deirdre points out. The leaping-dolphin fountain is yet another original feature that was painstakingly restored not once but twice. And this garden isn't really ours anymore, is it?

The flashes are still firing. The delivery guys start flexing muscle and mugging for the cameras, all thought of Ho-Ho-Ho-ing temporarily forgotten. Given the typical lack of hard news on Christmas Day, this over-the-top Christmas present from Daniel is probably already going viral.

Is it possible to refuse it? Or have it delivered to my parents' house in Atlanta? As of January 2, when we have to be out of here, that will be my only existing address.

"Listen, we can't really accept this. . . ." I begin.

"Sorry, lady." Santa flashes a big, toothy smile for the photographers and does a "hi, Mom" wave for the guy shooting video. "I've got to leave it. I got a premium for delivering tonight, but I don't get squat if I don't complete that delivery. My orders don't say anything about carrying it out back or nothing like that."

"Let them leave it here at the curb," Deirdre suggests. "If the city gets upset, we can just pretend we didn't know it was here."

"Right," Avery says. "We'll just act like Santa dropped it off."

"You know Dustin's going to love it. Tomorrow when Chase and his boys get here, we can figure out how to get it out back." This from my mother, whose glass always seems to be half-full.

"Give us a few more shots, ladies!" This time it's Bill who shouts. "We wasted the whole afternoon and most of the evening staking out the Vinoy Hotel." He names a restored Mediterranean Revival–style hotel in northeast St. Petersburg. "Someone said Barbara Streisand flew into town and was holed up in the penthouse. But it was just some female impersonator trying to promote his new e-book."

I do the whole turtle-pulling-into-its-shell thing and ignore them while I run in for my keys and angle the rental car up into the tag end of the driveway so that most of the curb is available for Dustin's present. Once the house clatters into place and the flatbed grinds off, we retreat back inside Bella Flora.

A text dings in on my mother's phone and I pick it up. "It's from Andrew and Dad. They got a late start out of Atlanta but should be here within the hour."

"Good," she says, smiling. "That's great." I expect her to head into the kitchen to see what she can put together for their dinner, or run out to the pool house to make sure everything's ready for them, but she shoves her glass toward Nikki and says, "I think that calls for a drink or two."

Mine aren't the only eyebrows that go up. Madeline Singer is many things. A heavy drinker isn't one of them. I can count the number of times I've seen her more than slightly tipsy on two fingers.

We head into the Casbah Lounge, which is one of the coolest rooms I've ever been in. It's small and intimate, with leaded glass windows, leather banquettes, and a riot of Moorish tile covering everything from the floor to the bar and the arched pillars and posts. Deirdre made sure it was restored to its original 1920s glamour, and whenever I'm in here I picture Bogie toasting Bacall and saying, "Here's looking at you, kid" while "As Time Goes By" plays hauntingly in the background.

Best of all, it's stocked with enough alcohol to survive a siege.

"We might as well drink up," Nikki says, stepping in behind the bar and opening a bottle of brandy.

Her pours are generous, but since none of us are going anywhere and tomorrow's Christmas, no one keeps track of who consumes what. I get the impression that my mother is drinking more with intent than enjoyment.

"To Bella Flora," Avery says.

We all drink to that.

"I'm going to miss her," Deirdre adds.

"Yeah. I never thought I'd say that when we were down on our knees refinishing the floors and sweating our asses off without air conditioning," Nikki says.

"Or sharing that one bathroom for most of the summer," I say.

"Or reglazing all those windows," Mom adds, and she should know. Bella Flora has about a bazillion windows, and she was the only one of us careful and patient enough to take on the tedious job of reglazing.

"I can't let myself think about strangers living in her," Avery says.

"I know." Nikki swallows the remainder of the brandy in her snifter and opens another bottle.

"I could barely make myself sign the contracts yesterday," my mother says. "But it was so generous of the new owner to allow us to stay through New Year's."

"I thought Chase was going to cry," Avery adds quietly.

"He wasn't the only one." Deirdre gives Avery a knowing look. This time when she rubs her arm it looks completely unintentional.

I smile at that. Avery's not exactly all girly girl, despite the fact that two networks have tried to present her that way. Chase Hardin looks better in his work boots and tool belt than a lot of guys do in a tux. But he has a soft spot for houses, especially spectacular historically significant ones like Bella Flora.

It's close to eleven when we hear a car out front. There's a soft knock on the door, and we all migrate into the foyer. My mom throws her arms around Andrew, who's in his junior year of college, then pecks my dad on both cheeks. I do the same and steal a quick look outside. Flashes go off as I close the front door.

"Where did the mini–Bella Flora come from?" Dad asks after he's greeted everyone. "I had to put the car in a metered space." My dad is tall and thin with hair that's turned more salt than pepper. He's rumpled from the drive. His tone is distinctly crotchety.

"It's Dustin's Christmas present from Daniel," I say.

"Kind of over-the-top, isn't it?" he grumbles.

"Not in movie-star terms," I say automatically, even though he's right and I have no reason to defend Daniel Deranian.

His expression is "bah humbug," but he doesn't argue the point. I don't think my father would have liked anyone I slept with. But he especially hates that Dustin's father is a married man who lied his way into my pants and had no interest in marrying me when I got pregnant. The fact that he gets paid a shitload of money for playacting and looking good is especially offensive.

"Hey, it could have been worse," Deirdre says. "It could have been a pony."

"We have a resident parking pass you can put on the dash." Avery retrieves the pass from the kitchen and hands it to my brother.

I almost ask him to tell the photographers outside that we're in for the night so they can go get some sleep. But then I think better of it. It's not the deer's job to tell the hunters when it's time to go home.

Nobody comments when my dad and brother carry

their things out to the pool house, but it still feels weird to me. "I can move Dustin and bunk in with Andrew if you want to stay in the house," I say to my dad.

"Oh, no. That's . . ." my mother begins.

". . . not necessary," my dad finishes. Strange. You never really think about your parents sleeping together until they don't.

When my mom asks if they're hungry, my brother perks up like he always does at the mention of food. None of us knows exactly where he puts it all, but his metabolism could probably light up the whole eastern seaboard. If it could be bottled we wouldn't have had to sell Bella Flora. Or put up with the network's heavy-handededness with *Do Over*.

My dad yawns. "I'm really whipped from the drive. I think I'm going to go on out and go to sleep."

He's gone before I can offer again. The rest of us head into the kitchen to see what's in the fridge, since we've had a lot more to drink than eat. Mini hot dogs and Cheez Doodles can only carry you so far.

There's a turkey just waiting to be stuffed for Christmas dinner tomorrow, but my mother pulls out the spiral-cut ham, a pound of deli roast beef, slices of provolone cheese, and a loaf of Italian bread from Casa del Pane just up the beach. We settle around the kitchen table with sandwiches. My "little" brother downs two huge glasses of milk in a gulp each and half the tin of homemade Christmas cookies that are passed around for dessert.

Upstairs, we all tiptoe around so we don't wake Dustin. In her room, I watch my mother set the alarm on the nightstand, climb into bed, and slip under the covers. "Good night, sweetheart." She yawns. "Sleep tight." She folds her hands across her chest and closes her eyes, but I can tell she's nowhere near falling asleep.

I hear Dustin's soft breathing from the portable crib and his occasional snuffle. Dustin's too young to understand the whole concept of getting up at the crack of dawn to see what Santa brought him, so I don't worry about setting an alarm or anything.

My mother's breathing evens out, but I still don't think she's asleep. I can practically feel her thinking beside me. I just don't know what she's thinking about.

I try to arrange my thoughts to maximize my dream potential. It's an exercise I read about once in a screenwriting book and that I've used when I'm in the middle of a shoot. When I check the clock, it's after midnight, so technically it's Christmas. But there are no sugar plums or candy canes dancing in my head. As I fall asleep, Max Golden makes an appearance—he's on a stage, doing a stand-up routine with his Millie, and he's holding the menorah we lit tonight. His smile is his megawatter, and his eyes twinkle with mischief.

Daniel elbows onstage beside them, sexy and stubble-faced. His hot dark eyes meet mine. His wife Tonja tries to join him onstage, but he tells her there's no room. She lets out a stream of profanities—and even in my half-conscious state I think how shocked her fans would be to find out what a total potty mouth she is. I regret having to edit out the video that Troy shot in South Beach of her swearing her movie-star guts out in front of my son. She's still swearing when Daniel reaches down to pick up Dustin then shoots me this saucy half wink. It would be a really touching moment if he didn't send an identical wink to somebody else off-camera; someone who's probably awestruck and beautiful and hasn't found out yet that she'll never beat out Tonja Kay, the rainbow of children she's adopted, and the lifestyle of the rich and famous that they live together.

My mother sighs beside me. My son snuffles in response. I teeter on the edge of sleep until almost one A.M. before I finally slip over into oblivion.

Merry Christmas to all, and to all a good night.

Chapter Five

Dustin's first word when he looks out the window and spies his "playhouse" on Christmas morning is "Buh-fora!" And while he smiles happily, he expresses no shock or surprise that an exact duplicate of Bella Flora sprang up on the front curb overnight. I wish I could remember being that age where magic can just happen.

The paparazzi are snapping away at the playhouse and the original behind it as soon as the sun is up, and I know I'm not going to be able to keep Dustin away from it. I toy with the idea of putting him in a disguise, but the paps all know there's only one toddler in this house. And I haven't been able to find a burqa in his size.

A crowd of neighbors and early bird tourists begins to form. A Pass-a-Grille traffic cop is trying to figure out how to hang a parking ticket on Bella Flora's mini-me.

In the kitchen, a big box of donuts is open on the reclaimed wood table. Avery's dunking a glazed chocolate in a cup of steaming coffee. I know it's not her first cup because she's smiling and talking—two things she doesn't do until the caffeine kicks in. I bought her a T-shirt for Christmas that reads, I DRINK COFFEE FOR YOUR PROTECTION, and I'm tempted to give it to her now.

Deirdre's eating a small cup of yogurt and is sitting as far away from the donuts as she can get. I'm guessing Nikki is out running; she's kind of like the post office that way—neither rain nor sleet nor . . . well, none of those things apply today, when the sun already looks like a big golden ball and the sky is a robin's-egg blue, but you get the idea. Nobody seems to be wearing more than a light layer or two, even though the Weather Channel is predicting that a cold front is headed our way.

My mother stands at the counter sipping coffee. The oven is already emitting mouthwatering turkey smells. My dad's reading the newspaper like there might be actual news in it and not just after Christmas sale ads. I try to imagine being with someone as long as they've been with each other, but my brain stalls out completely.

Dustin cries, "Gee-dad!" and launches himself into my father's lap, thrilled to see him but once again not surprised. So far in his world, absent fathers simply appear from time to time.

My mother walks over and kisses her grandson on the head. "Merry Christmas, Dustin." She smiles.

"Murree Krimas!" Dustin says and reaches his arms out to her. She scoops him up and settles him on her hip. There aren't a lot of people who can compete with my mother in Dustin's eyes.

There's a tap of a horn out front and a text dings in right afterward.

Chase and Jeff and the boys are out front. Are you ready to move the playhouse?

My dad leaves to get Andrew and I know it's going to take some time, and possibly a crowbar, to pry him out of bed.

"Do you want to stay inside with Dustin until we get it moved?" my mother asks me. She's untying her apron, and I notice that she's fully dressed for the day in black slacks and a bright red Christmas sweater with snowflakes and a snowman. I'm wearing the first thing I pulled on, and while I wouldn't mind staying here, I hate the idea of hiding. Especially on such a magnificent Christmas Day. "Hold on." I race upstairs and change into jeans and a *Do Over* sweatshirt. I refuse to dress up for the photographers, but if I can't avoid them I might as well plug the show.

My dad comes back with Andrew. My brother's face is shadowed with stubble, his eyes are barely open, and his clothes look slept in. In fact, he may still be asleep in a vertical, malleable sort of way. My mother puts a glass of orange juice in his hand and slips a pair of sunglasses on his face.

Deirdre meets us in the foyer. She's impeccably dressed in black knit pants and a royal blue tunic sweater. She looks like she might have hair and makeup people stashed in her room.

Avery takes one look at her and snorts. "Jesus," she says. "She can smell a photo op a mile away."

"I see no reason to face the media unprepared," Deirdre says. "They can only make us look bad if we allow it." She rubs her arm pointedly. "Perhaps you should go up and . . . dress."

"I *am* dressed." Avery's not hiding in those big over-size clothes anymore, but she's not into wardrobe co-ordination any more than I am. She has on jeans and a *Do Over* long-sleeved tee. "And that's not the media out there. That's a group of professional stalkers."

"Whose photographs will be on magazine and tab-loid covers. And could possibly be picked up for televi-sion." I can see that Deirdre considers stopping there but can't quite do it. "You remember when you ignored my warning on the way to South Beach and you ended up on-camera in that halter and those cutoffs?"

They both get that stubborn look on their faces. The set of their jaws is identical. As stressed as I feel about the horde outside and what we're supposed to do with Dustin's Christmas present, it takes some effort not to laugh.

We all tromp outside.

The flashes start firing. "Over here, Dustin! Look this way!"

"Give us a smile, Kyra!"

"Did Daniel send the minimansion?"

"Does Tonja know?"

"Will Daniel be here today to see Dustin?"

The whir of motor drives is almost as loud as the

shouted questions. Together they blot out the caw of gulls and the wash of the waves. They are like a pestilence. Put on this earth to torment anyone who has so much as a brush with fame.

"Will you leave the minimansion for the new owners?"

They know so much about all of us—too much. My heart is pounding in my chest but I do my best not to react.

Nicole arrives back from her run, sees the photographers, and tries not to huff and puff. Chase Hardin and his father, Jeff, who used to be in the construction business with Avery's father, and Chase's two sons are all over six feet, which makes them only slightly taller than the playhouse's gabled roof. Chase slips an arm around Avery and tucks her close to his side. I get this weird little jab of awareness. All Dustin has is me. How will I protect him from all of this? What will he think of being a celebrity's illegitimate child when he's old enough to understand?

But as I think this, everyone assembles around the outside of the playhouse, kind of like a human shield, so that Dustin, who's chortling with glee, can go inside and check it out. I go with him and I don't even have to hunch over. We both giggle. There's no floor, but the inside walls are plastered and painted like a real house; there's a faux fireplace on one wall. It feels warm and safe. If there weren't a mob of photographers outside, it would be perfect.

I'm peeking out one of the floor-to-ceiling windows, trying to see past our human wall, when I spot a familiar figure. It's Troy Matthews, the Lifetime cameraman. At the moment he's standing behind the outer ring of paparazzi. The sun glints off his shaggy blond hair. His video camera is perched on one broad shoulder. I spent the last few months editing *Do Over* with him, but when I left Nashville yesterday morning he never said a word about being here today. The rat.

I'm careful not to look his way, but I won't be able to ban him from the house or the grounds like I can the others. He's kind of like a vampire that you have to invite in.

I see Avery and Chase conferring. She comes inside. "Are you guys okay?"

"Yeah."

"Good. Here's the plan."

At Chase's cue, I pull Dustin into my arms and hold on tight. Everyone else grabs a window opening, a wrought-iron balcony, a cupola, a column—any protrusion they can use as a handhold. On the count of three, they lift the house off the ground. The house bobs up and down as they carry it, like an army of ants carrying a picnic basket, up over the curb and across a lot-sized patch of grass strewn with sand and scrub, a sort of no-man's-land that separates Bella Flora from the path that leads to the jetty, fishing pier, and beach.

There's a lot of grumbling and laughing as they try to synchronize their movements and compensate for their disparate heights. I just hold on to Dustin and do my best to keep pace so that we don't trip on the uneven ground or get flattened if they drop it or whacked by a wall if we fall out of step. Once we've made it around Bella Flora, the house comes to a bobbling halt. I dart out with Dustin and watch while Avery and Chase confer about its placement. It ends up next to Dustin's beloved sandbox, smack up against the loggia, with its back to the gulf.

"If we were getting to stay here, all we'd need is a fence down the property line and Dustin could play all he wanted," my mother says.

Of course, it would have to be a see-through fence, which would sort of defeat the purpose. This will never be a gated property. No one in his right mind would block 150 feet of prime waterfront or the spectacular view out over the gulf.

The paparazzi reposition themselves three hundred yards away as required—do they have tape measures in their heads? This puts them on the far edge of the no-man's-land, and I hope they get stickers and seagull poop all over them. But the playhouse does help block their view of the loggia a little.

I watch Dustin race in and out of the playhouse. He carries a favorite fire truck inside and then some other toys. Troy sets up his camera on a tripod and shoots. I've mostly given up trying to hide Dustin from the network camera. My famous child is one of the reasons we have a television show at all. There's no getting around it. And the show's too important to all of us for any one of us to walk.

"You could have told me you were coming to shoot today."

"I figured you knew." Troy is tall and good-looking, and although I don't plan to tell him this any time soon, he's a really good cameraman. If we needed one besides me, which we don't, he'd definitely be a keeper. But we set out to do a renovation show, and when we arrived in South Beach last spring, we found out that the network had turned it into a reality series with Troy's camera focused on us.

"It's Christmas Day." He locks his camera down, leaving it aimed at the door of the playhouse to catch Dustin as he runs in and out. I hate that there's nothing I can do about it. "Could there be a better time to let you know where the next season of *Do Over* will be shot?" He says this casually as if it's not one more slap in the face. Part of the network's strategy has been not revealing the house we'll be renovating or its address until we arrive in the city they've selected. Which puts a real crimp in the ability to prep the renovation and adds a whole unnecessary layer of stress and panic that Troy gets to capture on camera.

"Do you want to give me a small hint?" I ask because at the moment one more thing that I don't know and have no control over could push me over the edge.

"They didn't tell me," he says, and I look at his face to see if this is true. "They think I've been turned by the 'enemy.' That I have an unhealthy attraction to you."

I have no idea what to say to this. He did invite me to edit with him, which Lisa Hogan, the network head, whose nickname is "the chief bitch in charge," didn't like. And he did make fifteen minutes of the worst of our infighting disappear. Sort of like that seven minutes of Watergate conversation that took place in Nixon's oval office that was accidentally erased.

"All I have is a sealed envelope, which is supposed to be opened when you're all together and on-camera." He loosens the shot so that he can follow Dustin through the playhouse windows. I grit my teeth.

"Time to open presents!" Mom pokes her head out to yell. Everyone troops inside. The smell of turkey infuses the air. Christmas music is playing. Mom has a tray of orange juices plus a couple of bottles of champagne to turn them into mimosas sitting on the game table. A platter of donuts, mini cinnamon buns, and muffins sits nearby.

There are a ton of presents piled under the tree. Even though it's supposed to be in the seventies today, someone has lit a fire in the fireplace. We start to tear through the presents. In minutes there's wrapping paper and ribbon all over the floor. Troy is filming, and for once I don't care because it leaves me free to help Dustin open his gifts. My son is all about tools and transportation and everyone knows it, so he gets a set of toddler-sized tools tucked into an adorable tool belt from Avery and Deirdre, a truck pulling a speedboat on a trailer from the Hardins, and a whole fire station complete with a pimped-out fire truck and crew from my mom, dad, and brother. I save the kiddie video camera with its eyepiece and a zoom lens that I bought for him for last, and my heart does this weird kind of stutter when he swings it right up onto his shoulder like he's seen me do a thousand times. I look up and see Troy moving in for a close-up; he and Dustin look like dueling cameramen. I'm about to give Troy some shit about it when I notice that his lips, which are about all you can see behind the camera, are curved up into a genuine smile.

I look down at my son, who's so excited he doesn't know what to play with first, and then around the room. I'm touched that everyone—even the teenagers—brought something for Dustin. He does belong to all of us in a way I don't think a child with two parents can. This is the village that is helping me raise my child.

"Wow!" Chase grins when Avery opens her present from Deirdre. The lingerie is incredibly skimpy, the barest wisps of pink silk, nude satin, and black lace. The chance of her actually wearing any of these things seems pretty close to zero. She spent most of our time in South Beach hiding in baggy clothes so the network couldn't focus on her chest all the time like the last network did. Her favorite accessories are the pink hard hat her father gave her when she was a little girl and her father's tool belt, which has extra holes punched in so it doesn't fall down around her hips.

"I think this is the same pink as your hard hat." Chase nods at a silky thong and waggles his eyebrows. "Thanks, Deirdre!"

"This was supposed to be *my* present," Avery complains. "Not his."

"It's for both of you," Deirdre replies. "But you don't have to wear any of it if you don't want to."

"Even better." Chase grins. "Here." He hands Avery a crudely wrapped box that clearly doesn't hold lingerie. "I'm going to picture you using my present while you're wearing one of Deirdre's."

We're all watching now. Avery rips off the paper. Her face lights up as she pulls out a shiny new drill and—be still my heart—a tape measure. Apparently it's possible to go through these items regularly.

"I love them!" Avery exclaims. "My old ones are on their last legs."

"Your turn." Avery hands him a box.

Chase makes quick work of the wrapping paper. He

holds up what looks like some ancient instrument of torture.

"What is it?" Nicole asks as we all stare at the U-shaped piece of wood with a knob at one end and a squared pointy thing on the other.

"It's an antique brass-plated brace," Chase's father, Jeff, says. "It looks English."

"It's gorgeous." Chase runs a hand over the worn wood, turns it gently in his hands. "I've been lusting after one of these for years."

They're handling their tools intimately and staring into each other's eyes. Chase leans down and whispers something in her ear and she blushes. I'm surprised nobody tells them to "get a room."

"How incredibly romantic," Deirdre says drily. "You are clearly and irrevocably your father's daughter."

"The last time I got that excited about a gift, it had four wheels and a convertible top," Nikki says. I wonder if she's referring to her classic Jag.

There's a flash of light on camera lens and I see Troy framing a shot of my mother, who's handing a fresh mimosa to Deirdre. Troy turns smoothly, panning the camera across the room to my dad, who's just kind of staring into the fire. My parents have been through some really rough times in the last year and a half; neither of them behaved in quite the way I expected— my dad fell apart, and my mom was a rock—but they're an inspiration. Not that I have any real options or anything, but I'm not planning to marry anyone who's not in it for the long haul.

My mom and Nicole and Deirdre head to the kitchen. After asking Avery to keep an eye out for Dustin, I join them. I love the kitchen, with its reclaimed wood and tile and its glass-fronted cabinets. Deirdre can be a bit much at times, but she's one hell of a designer. Bella Flora and The Millicent down in Miami wouldn't be anywhere near as spectacular without her input, and she can talk anyone except Avery into pretty much anything. The furnishings and artwork that fill Bella Flora now are on loan for staging purposes. The mystery owner bought it all, which is a win-win for the design firms and stores who installed everything. And it says something about the buyer, though I'm not sure if it says he's lazy but has good taste or just has more money than he or she knows what to do with.

"Oh, good. Will you help set the table?" My mother gives me a hug and a smile, and I see that she's brought a tablecloth and her good silver from home. Nicole,

Deirdre, and I cart everything into the dining room and start laying it all out while my mother bastes the turkey and pops the sweet potato soufflé into the oven. It looks like a total repeat of Thanksgiving, which was also Dustin's birthday, and I wonder if she just made double then and had everything waiting in the freezer. That's so Maddie: the perfect homemaker and mother. I don't have a Martha Stewart thought or bone in my body. No home, no matter how spectacular, is as exciting to me as a film set. Even though none of my film and television experiences have turned out remotely the way I hoped.

Chapter Six

Our Realtor, John Franklin, and his wife arrive at 11:30, and we sit down to Christmas "dinner" at noon. John Franklin is somewhere in his eighties with a ruff of white hair and a long face dominated by the droopy brown eyes of a basset hound. He's lived on St. Pete Beach since God was a boy and is full of information about Pass-a-Grille, which began as a small fishing village, and Bella Flora, which was built in 1928, when *he* was a boy.

All of us except my father adore him, but even we are surprised that he found a buyer for Bella Flora. And that that buyer paid almost full asking price. His wife,

Renée, is younger and more robust than John, but they sit close to each other and lean even closer. It's possible that this is more about maintaining balance than affection—John does use a cane—but it's hard to miss the fact that they gaze adoringly at each other. My parents do not.

"The replica playhouse is beautifully done," John says when he's cleaned his plate. "Maybe we should have left it out front with a matching sold sign outside."

This is too depressing to contemplate.

"I can't even let myself think about how much it cost," Chase says. "I probably could have built a real house from scratch for that. Or renovated another Bella Flora."

Except there is no other Bella Flora, and all of us know it. Bella Flora brought us all together and she's practically a member of the family.

"It's a waste of money, if you ask me," my dad says. "I guess when you have that much you don't even give it a thought."

I can't meet his eyes. Ever since he lost everything to Malcolm Dyer, he seems to have a major issue with anyone who's managed to hold on to their money.

The cut glass chandelier throws shards of light

glinting off the silver and spotlights the acres of food my mother has prepared. Despite the fact that we have thirteen and a half people chowing down, three of whom are teenage boys, it could take hours of eating to even make a dent. My mother's in her glory. Dustin's already rubbing his eyes and is in major need of a nap. I'm reaching for a third homemade biscuit when my phone rings.

The name Deranian appears on the screen. Even now, after Daniel's proved himself untrustworthy and somewhat lacking in moral fiber, the sight of his name on my caller ID creates this embarrassing rush of excitement, which I try to hide. He's probably calling to wish Dustin a Merry Christmas. Or to make sure his present got here. I'm definitely going to give him some shit about his extravagance, but the truth is I like that he wants to do nice things for our child. He's a hard man to say no to, even from a distance. It can be even harder to separate the roles he plays on-screen from his behavior in real life.

I leave the dining room so that I can talk to him in private, but it's not Daniel on the other end.

"What the fuck do you think you're doing?" Tonja Kay's voice is cold and hard.

It's almost impossible to reconcile the actress's angelic face and silky on-screen voice with the way she swears like a truck driver in real life. *Fuck* is her go-to adjective, adverb, and noun. My mother has lectured her on this, and I have to think her publicity people must spend a ton of time and money trying to keep her limited—and ugly—vocabulary out of the tabloids, but she really doesn't give a shit. The fact that she talks this way around her children is horrifying. The fact that Troy got video of her doing it with a vengeance in front of mine is the only thing that prevents her from taking Dustin—and *Do Over*—away from me.

I want to hang up, but Tonja Kay is a foul-mouthed force of nature. Like a tornado or a hurricane, she sucks you in against your will. If she knocks you down she'll roll right over you.

I walk out onto the loggia, where I breathe deeply and try to calm myself with the view of sky and water. It's a gorgeous, un-Christmas-like day, the kind that belongs on a postcard with the words *Wish You Were Here* scrawled across the bottom.

"I don't know what the fuck he thinks he's doing buying that fucking house!" Tonja Kay shouts.

My eyes move to the replica of Bella Flora. Of course,

she just hates that Daniel sent his son anything this extravagant. Her children are all adopted from troubled third-world countries, and Daniel's other biological children—he isn't exactly a poster boy for marriage or monogamy—are girls. The fact that Dustin is Daniel's only biological son drives her absolutely insane.

A boat slows in the pass and I see the glint of a telephoto lens. I turn my back as she says, "I mean, he has a fucking lot of fucking nerve!"

I sigh and wish I could hand off the phone, but I can't go running to my mother or anyone else to fight my battles for me. And, frankly, it's hard to take this conversation seriously, because although the playhouse might have been outrageously expensive, Daniel Deranian and Tonja Kay earn more millions per picture than I can count. I don't think the playhouse is going to bankrupt either of them.

Tonja Kay—I can never think of her by only one name—rants on. It's hard to tune out when there's that much bad language, which I guess is her goal. I see more lenses glinting—the paparazzi have gotten into position in hopes that one of us will be stupid enough to come outside. For just a second I consider putting Tonja Kay on speakerphone and inviting them closer, but I'm saving Troy's video for emergency purposes. And besides, today is Christmas.

She's just finished calling Daniel some nasty names I don't even know the meaning of. I hear the word *cunt* and know she means me. I've definitely had enough. "Listen, it's been great talking with you and all," I say with as much sarcasm as I can squeeze in, "but it is a holiday and I have to go now."

I'm about to hang up when she shrieks, "I don't even *want* your piece-of-crap house. Who names a house Bella fucking Flora?"

"What?" I ask. A shiver runs down my spine despite the sunny seventy-five degrees when I register what she said. "What did you say?"

"I said, I don't know why the fuck Daniel bought that stupid fucking house without telling me."

Another stream of curses fly from her mouth, but I barely notice.

Daniel is the mystery buyer? Daniel has bought Bella Flora for *his* family?

I pace the loggia, my eyes shut to the beautiful day. I hear boat motors and the whine of a WaveRunner. Someone's shouting for me to "Look this way" and asking, "What's your mom serving for Christmas dinner?" but it's just noise.

The biscuits turn to rocks in my stomach.

"Aren't you going to fucking say anything?" Tonja Kay demands.

I can barely think, let alone speak, so I just keep pacing, even though I'm going to look like a crazy woman in the tabloids. *Please, God. Not them in Bella Flora. Let it be anyone but them.*

I look in horror now at the playhouse. Did Daniel send it as some sort of sick joke?

My silence has given Tonja Kay time to cool down. A taunting tone steals into her voice. "Of course, now that I think about it, since we own it, I can bring my contractor and designer in to fix whatever you've done to it." I don't respond—I can't—so she continues. "I saw this great indoor pool on *Million-Dollar Rooms.*"

I hang up while she's cackling in my ear about how many walls they'll have to rip out to fit in the pool. I stare out over the pass, trying not to picture Tonja Kay and her brood and the governesses—one for each child—swimming in what is currently the salon and tramping all over the house that we brought back to life and that did the same for us.

I have this ridiculous image of Avery chaining herself to the front door and the rest of us lying down across Beach Road, blocking the driveway and the front steps to keep them from entering Bella Flora. But there aren't enough of us. And we've already closed. I don't think you're allowed to change your mind once that's happened and money has changed hands. And it's not as if anyone has enough money to give it back even if we could.

Finally I go back inside. But I can't bring myself to tell anyone that Daniel has bought Bella Flora. Not today; not on Christmas. I sit and stare at the slice of apple pie that someone's put on my plate. When I feel everyone looking at me, I force myself to take a bite. It tastes bitter on my tongue and in my mouth. It tastes like disappointment. And regret.

I ignore my mother's concerned looks and the questions in her eyes while we clear the table and load the dishwasher. The guys are out on the beach throwing a football around—how do they get away with that? Everyone's looking at me by the time we finish in the kitchen, but I scoop up Dustin and announce that we're going upstairs to take a nap. No one argues with this. Around here Dustin's naptime is almost as sacred as our sunset toasts.

Upstairs I lie on the bed staring up into the ceiling. Beside me Dustin's breathing grows regular and his thumb finds its way into his mouth. I wish I could suck my thumb or twirl my hair like I did when I was his age, but I'm a grown woman now and those comforts are no longer available. Counting sheep and trying to regulate my breathing as if I'm in a yoga class are a bust. So I just lie there with my thoughts flittering wherever they choose. I think about trying to reach Daniel to ask him why he bought Bella Flora, but it doesn't really matter why. And the only time he really listens to me is when he thinks he has a shot at getting me back into bed.

I must fall asleep at some point, because I wake to Dustin's chubby fingers cupping my chin and his face pressed to mine. I open my eyes to stare into his. "Beeeech." He says this expectantly. "Castle?"

I look out the window and see that it's late afternoon, which means we've been asleep for a couple of hours. Sunset can't be far off.

"Okay." I throw off the covers, splash water on my

face in the bathroom, change Dustin's diaper, and carry him down the back stairs. The kitchen is empty, and I fill a sippy cup with juice and pour some Goldfish crackers into a Ziploc snack bag. I hear what sounds like my father's voice in the salon. He pauses occasionally and I don't hear anyone respond, so I guess he must be on the phone.

"Hey, what's going on?" Suddenly Troy is in the kitchen doorway, video camera on his shoulder. When he reaches us, he gives Dustin a high five with his free hand. Dustin's face breaks into a smile. Even down in Miami, when I hated Troy and he disapproved of me, he and Dustin had a mutual admiration thing going. Still, he's shooting for the network, and his assignment does not include making us look good.

"Nothing. Where is everybody?"

"The guys took a break from bowl games to go out on the beach. Your mom and the others are out on the pool deck, waiting for sunset."

"Beeeeech," Dustin says, reaching toward Troy. It's a money shot, I know, and there's nothing I can do about it.

"I can take him out on the beach to hang with the guys," Troy says.

Our sunset is a network camera–free event. I'm the only one allowed to shoot them. Usually there are no males, except Dustin, allowed. I only hesitate for a minute. Chase and my brother will help keep an eye out, and I know Troy will shield Dustin as much as possible from the paparazzi if only to protect the network's interests. "Okay. But don't let him eat sand. Or drink the salt water. Or . . ."

"I've got it under control." Dustin reaches for him again, and I let Troy tuck him into the crook of his free arm. Which has the added advantage of making it almost impossible for him to get a good shot of my son. "We'll be up after the sun goes down. I've got to get footage of you opening the envelope with the next *Do Over* location."

Of course he does. I say nothing, but it's yet another unwelcome reminder that I have almost zero control over the show I created.

When they're gone I putter for a little bit, trying to push back the image of Tonja Kay in this kitchen or presiding over cocktails in the Casbah Lounge. Or worse, ripping them both out in order to wedge a pool in their place. I breathe deeply for a while, trying to steady and slow my thoughts, but it doesn't work any better while I'm vertical than it did while I was trying to nap. There's no point in getting worked up about Daniel owning Bella Flora. We'd be leaving her behind, no matter who bought her. And there's always the chance that Dustin will get to spend some time here with his father.

I drink a Coke and pick at some leftovers until I feel ready to go outside and come up with 'one good thing.' I hang my video camera over my shoulder. As I leave the kitchen I realize my father's still on the phone. His voice is pitched low, but I catch a few words and phrases.

"I know," he says. "But I'll be back soon, and we can celebrate then." He chuckles, which is so not a Steve Singer sound that I stop dead in my tracks. When I look through the French doors, he's got this kind of goofy smile on his face and I realize that it's affection I hear in his voice.

"I've missed you. But I'll be back in Atlanta soon," he practically coos. It's then that I know for sure that he's talking to a woman. And that woman is most definitely not my mother.

Chapter Seven

I'm still standing in the hall outside the salon when he gets off the phone. I tell myself not to say anything. That this is not my business. That I should just erase what I heard from my memory banks and go outside to toast the sunset. But I'm a cameraperson, not an actor. And this is my father, not some stranger. The next thing I know I'm in the salon and moving toward my dad. Who's got a perfect view of my mom and the others gathered near the pool with drinks in their hands. So that she couldn't possibly overhear him or catch him unaware. The shit!

He sees me and smiles, but I see guilt stamped across

his face. Too bad they don't have big red letter *A*s for men. At the moment I'd be glad to nail it to his forehead.

"Hi, kitten. Did you have a good nap?"

I don't trust myself to speak. I nod, my eyes pinned to his face while I try to think of any other explanation for what I've overheard than the obvious one.

"Is everything all right?" His brow is furrowed as if with concern. But I don't trust any of his expressions now. He fell apart when he lost all our money and his job, and my mother was forced to step up and try to put our lives back together. And this is how he repays her? By screwing around with someone else?

"I don't know," I say. "Is it?" I glance through the floor-to-ceiling windows and see my mother laugh.

He shrugs. "It's Christmas, and pretty soon it'll be a brand-new year. There's nothing like the prospect of a fresh start."

He looks so smug and happy that I want to gag. I *am* gagging on all the things I want to say. I feel like I did when I was five and the boy next door told me there was no Santa Claus *or* Easter Bunny.

How could you? I think but do not ask. Because I don't think I can bear to hear his excuses. And if he admits that he's having an affair, there'll be no taking it back.

Do all men cheat? Is it just a matter of time? Something that's hardwired into their DNA, a time bomb set to go off sometime after the day they say *I do* but before they keel over?

But I don't care about other men right now. I only care about my father. I had an affair with a married man even though I knew it wasn't right. But it would have been even worse if Tonja Kay weren't the nasty person she is. If she were . . . my mom.

"Right. Well, I should get outside." I can't meet his eyes, which is stupid since he's the one who's doing something wrong.

When I get outside my mother pats the chair next to her and Nikki hands me a glass of red wine. Temperatures are set to drop and now that the sun's on its way down it is a bit cold for a frozen drink. Avery's fingers are orange from Cheez Doodles. Deirdre's sticking out her chin over something. "You're just in time," my mother says. "We've been holding off on our 'one good things' until you got here."

I take a sip of wine and study my mother's face. She looks happy and relaxed despite having cooked and served a major Christmas dinner. But then, she didn't hear her husband on the phone just now telling some other woman how much he misses her. And she doesn't know that Daniel Deranian is the new owner of Bella Flora.

Normally I'd be shooting the sunset and our "one good thing" ritual, but I just sit and listen as the toasts begin, wondering what in the hell I'm going to say. *I'm glad my mother doesn't know my father's cheating on her* doesn't seem quite right. Neither does *Maybe Tonja Kay won't do too much damage to Bella Flora.*

I'm still thinking damage control when Deirdre says, "I'm glad Avery didn't burn the lingerie I gave her. And I believe if she actually wears it good things will happen."

"Oh God," Avery groans. "You are not going to turn me sleeping with Chase into your good thing."

Deirdre's eyes flash in protest, but she wisely stays silent.

"You're sleeping with Chase?" Nicole asks in faux shock, which cracks everyone up and lightens the mood. As badly as my gut is churning, I can't help laughing.

"Ha, look who's talking," Avery shoots back. "At least I'm not sleeping with the FBI." She licks the cheese off her fingers with a *Take that* kind of look.

"I'm not sleeping with the whole FBI. Just one agent." Nikki smiles wickedly. "And there's not a whole lot of sleeping going on anyway."

When I first met Nicole Grant she looked so sophisticated and la-di-da, even in her designer running clothes, but underneath is an iron will and a ramrod of a backbone. I think Agent Joe Giraldi has his work cut out for him.

"That's your good thing?" Avery challenges.

Nicole looks like she's going to argue, but she says, "Yes, I guess it is. My brother may be a greedy convicted felon and Heart, Inc. may be pretty much dead and buried. But good sex is a good thing."

We all drink to that. I think about picking up my camera and getting a couple of shots, but I don't. I try to keep my video honest, and honest is the last thing I feel like I can be right now.

"I don't see Agent Giraldi bringing someone he just has sex with home to meet his family," my mother observes. Nicole doesn't respond, but she does pour herself another glass of wine. Normally, I'd be zooming in for a close-up, but I still don't pick up my camera. All I can think is that my dad seems to be having good sex with someone else.

"Kyra?" Deirdre asks, but I shake my head. I'm definitely not ready yet.

"Okay, then that leaves you, Maddie," Deirdre says.

My mother smiles and makes eye contact with each of us like she always does. "My good thing, my very best thing, is the same as last night. Having you all here to celebrate the holiday in my favorite place on earth is incredible. Even if it is the last time." She raises her glass. "Here's to the new owners of Bella Flora. May they love her and appreciate her every bit as much as we do."

I raise my glass to my lips, but I don't drink. There's no way I can possibly swallow right now. I'm trying my hardest not to even think about Daniel, Tonja Kay, and their entourage tromping around the house that changed all of our lives; I'm definitely not going to drink to it. I also try not to think about my father and how he's betraying my mother, actually betraying all of us. That's a lot of things not to think about. I feel warm and overdressed, even though it's cold out here now that the sun has gone down. I can actually feel my body temperature rising. If I were a teapot, I'd be close to a boil.

"I can hardly wait for the new year and the fresh start that it brings," my mother continues, eerily echoing what my father said. "We'll all have a clean slate to write on. There's so much opportunity to . . ."

"Oh, my God!" I cut her off midsentence. I just can't take it. "Are you serious?"

My mother looks at me. Her expression is one of concern, not anger, which makes me feel even worse. If, in fact, that's possible. "Are you completely blind?" I ask. "Or don't you care that Daddy is . . ."

"No, Kyra," she interrupts me. "This isn't a good time to talk about your father."

There's a warning note in her voice, but everything's roiling inside me, looking for a way out. "I heard Dad on the phone," I say in a rush. "He was talking to another woman!"

No one says anything as I spew out the rest. "He told her that he missed her. That he can't wait to get back to Atlanta." I barely stop long enough to breathe. "After everything he's done, after everything he's put you through, I can't believe you're letting him cheat on you."

I can't believe I'm losing it like this, either, but I can't seem to stop. I know I should have waited until we were alone to bring this up—or not brought it up at all—but I just can't handle it alone. I look at my mother's face.

She's upset but not shocked. I look at Deirdre and Avery and Nicole. Their discomfort is obvious, but they're not shocked either.

Everyone already knows. Everyone but me.

"It's not what you think," my mother says while everyone else tries to look as if they're not there or at least not listening. "It's . . ."

"It's what?" My internal censor has checked out, and I'm practically shrieking like a child. Which is what I feel like. Small and irrational and helpless and unable to control what's happening to my life as I know it. "He has a girlfriend and you don't care?" I'm mortally offended on my mother's behalf. She deserves so much more than this. But I'm also mad at her for letting him get away with this. I can't stand that I'm about to cry.

"Kyra, sweetie. It's all right. Everything's okay."

"How can you say that?" I watched my mother take on the whole load for our family when my father fell apart. I've been surprised and inspired by her unexpected strength. I want her to storm inside and threaten to cut off his balls. And at the same time I want her to smooth things over. To fix this like she's always fixed everything else. "This is definitely not okay!" And never would be again.

"Kyra, honey. Your father is seeing someone. But that's because we're already living . . . separately." She swallows and I think about her insistence that Dustin and I stay in her bedroom. The physical distance they've maintained that I've been trying not to notice. "Because we're getting a divorce."

My hand drops to my video camera and my fingers wrap around the grip. I wish I could pick it up and hide behind it. "But why didn't you tell me? How could you not tell me?"

"We didn't want to ruin the holiday, sweetheart. We wanted you and Andrew and Dustin to have this last Christmas with both of us. As a family."

Tears fill my eyes, turning everything soft and out of focus. My parents, who've been married for twenty-six years, are getting a divorce. "He's divorcing you? But, why would he want a divorce now? How can he do this to you?"

"He's not *doing* this to me, honey. He's giving me what I want. I asked for the divorce."

Without speaking, Avery, Nikki, and Deirdre get up and begin to carry things inside. Vaguely I realize the sky is darkening.

"But I don't understand. You've been together for

so long. You've been through so much. All the hardest stuff is over. Dad's back on his feet. You're fifty-one. Why would you want to be alone now? I mean, that's just . . ."

"Silly?" she asks quietly. "You think I'm too old to bother?"

"No," I say, but of course that's exactly what I think. "No, of course not."

She sighs. "At my age you start thinking not only about the length of time you have left, but the quality of that life. And despite everything we've been through—or maybe because of it—I can't be myself—the self I am now anyway—with your father." Her smile is apologetic. It's me she's worried about.

I hear the finality in her voice and I can't hold back the tears anymore. They pour out of my eyes and skid down my cheeks.

My mother wraps her arms around me. "Oh, Kyra. Honey. I'm so sorry." She wipes a tear off my cheek and I look up at her, but her face is a blur. "I'll always love your father in certain ways, and I'll always be grateful to him for giving me you and Andrew."

I'm crying full-out now.

"He'll always be your father. And Dustin's grandfather." She pauses. "But I think I deserve to make the most of the time I have left, don't you?"

I nod because I know I'm supposed to, but I feel like someone ripped a hole in my chest the size of the Holland Tunnel. I just can't process this on top of everything else.

I hate that I'm crying, but it's a lot harder to stop than it is to start. "I just feel like there isn't anything I can do about . . . anything."

"Oh, sweetie." She brings her forehead to mine. "There's nothing to be done. Change is the only constant, and there's no point in wasting time and energy trying to fight it. There's just acceptance and moving forward."

I sniff and nod, my forehead pressing into hers. My mother has turned into this font of New Age wisdom when all I really want are the pancakes with the smiley face formed with chocolate bits and peanut-butter-and-jelly sandwiches shaped like stars. Is that too selfish for words?

She unwraps her arms from around me but holds on to my hand. I don't know if she signals them that it's okay or they've been watching and waiting for the right moment, but Avery, Nikki, and Deirdre come back bearing more wine. I try not to be mad that they knew about my parents before I did. Timing isn't really the point.

Nicole fills everyone's glasses and I take a long drink.

"Are you okay?" Avery asks.

I nod even though I'm not. The tears are on intermittent now, but I can't seem to locate the off switch. It's small of me. I think I've already used the words childish and selfish, but I can't help it. I'm both of those things. I just can't bear to be the only one dealing with bad news. So I raise my glass. "I guess this is as good a time as any to share some news."

I have their attention now and I don't let myself stop and think about whether this is the best time to share it. "Daniel bought Bella Flora. He's the mystery buyer. Tonja Kay called today to tell me how pissed off she is about it."

I see the shock and horror on their faces, but I'm beyond caring. "She can't wait to get her hands on it. She and her designer." Deirdre once worked for Tonja Kay, but not anymore. "She's thinking about gutting the first floor so that they can build an indoor pool."

No one speaks or moves. No one even lifts a glass to her lips or so much as swallows. I'm not sure anyone is breathing.

"So I guess my one good thing is that we won't be here when he moves Tonja Kay, their kids, and her interior designer into the place she referred to as *Bella fucking Flora*."

Chapter Eight

We're sitting in a stunned silence when Troy walks up from the beach. Once the sunset is complete, the camera-free zone ceases to exist, so his camera is on his shoulder. The men are right behind him. My father is holding Dustin's hand. Chase and his father and sons are arranged around him. Andrew brings up the rear. They look like a batch of linemen in a protective formation around a miniature quarterback.

The pack of paparazzi straggle up the path behind them and plant themselves in the no-man's-land of scrub and sand that lies between Bella Flora and the jetty. Apparently no real celebrities or celebrity look-alikes have popped up in the Tampa Bay area. We will have to do.

I brush my lips across Dustin's sandy forehead and brush a dark curl back out of his eye, but I don't meet my father's eye when he hands Dustin to me, and I don't speak when Troy begins to herd us inside for the grand announcement of the location of our next *Do Over*. I'm not sure how it's possible to seethe and go numb at the same time, but that's what I'm doing. I am an emotional Oreo cookie—hard and crumbly on the outside, soft and seething in the middle.

Avery goes up on her tiptoes to whisper something in Chase's ear.

He swears, and I know she's told him about Daniel buying Bella Flora. Chase poured his heart, his skills, and his money into both of her renovations. I hope Avery's spared him the part about the indoor pool. And that I'm not around when he tells his dad.

"All right, everybody." Troy continues to herd us toward the house, filming as we go. "We're going to shoot the reveal in the salon."

Just before the doors close behind us, I hear Nigel and Bill and the paparazzi at their backs begging for one more shot. A smile. Anything. Even a mooning from my brother or one of the Hardin boys would probably make their day. But I don't turn around. They've had every bit of the golden hour when the light is best to get shots of Dustin on the beach. That's as close to a Christmas present as they're going to get from me.

Inside the lights are still twinkling on the tree. Opened presents lie all over the floor around it. Troy motions Mom, Avery, Chase, Deirdre, Nicole, and me to the sectional near the fireplace, then sets his camera on a tripod across from us, which will allow him to include the tree, the presents, and the rest of the group in the background. It's exactly where I would have set up if I'd been shooting this, but I will never tell him that.

I breathe deeply and settle Dustin on my lap, trying to focus on what's happening, but my mind is filled with images of Tonja Kay wreaking foul-mouthed revenge on our poor defenseless Bella Flora and of my family, which will only have one of my parents in it at a time. My reality has altered so much in the last twenty-four hours that I hardly recognize it. I'm afraid if someone looks at me the wrong way I'm going to start crying again.

I want to be anywhere but here. I'd be heading there right now, except that "anywhere but here" is not an option.

Troy locks down the camera, makes a small adjustment, and hands Avery the sealed envelope.

"Are you guys ready?" Avery asks. Her smile is uneven. Her hands tremble so badly that the envelope wobbles. My hands are clasped around Dustin's stomach, which has the dual purpose of keeping him semistill and disguising my own trembling. He's busy twirling the propeller of a wooden toy helicopter and kicking one of his legs against mine. He couldn't care less about the camera, but then people have been aiming them at him since he was born.

Avery licks her lips as she tears open the flap and I realize how dry mine are. My mother reaches a hand over and rests it on mine, but I don't meet her eyes. We're about to find out where we're going next—the network could theoretically send us anywhere in the world—but I still feel oddly half-numb. My emotional Novocain is starting to wear off.

Troy waves one hand above the lens until I look up. His lips stretch into a smile. He points at them and then at me. I smile and try to look eager and engaged. This is business. I have to be professional. No matter how much I resent Troy being first camera and the unpleasant reality TV turn *Do Over* has taken, none of us can afford to walk away from a network television series. I wear what I hope is an expectant look on my face as Avery's eyes skim over the card. All of us zone back in from wherever we've escaped to as she begins to speak.

"Your next *Do Over* will start in May," she intones. "When you turn the home of an extremely high-profile individual into a bed-and-breakfast." Avery looks up and I can tell that like the rest of us she's trying to figure out just how high a profile we're talking. Is it a politician? A movie star? A relative of Mother Teresa?

"That home . . ." She flips the card over then hesitates as if waiting for a drum roll. ". . . is located somewhere in the Florida Keys."

There's a beat of silence and then the guys hoot their approval. Without urging from Troy, they come toward us, talking fast.

"I've been down there by boat and car," Chase says. "The fishing and diving are great. But May's the beginning of the rainy season. It's hot and humid as hell there in the summer, and the mosquitoes are as big as helicopters."

"Hurrykopter!" Dustin says, spinning the wooden propeller.

"One of my roommates went to Key West last year for spring break," Andrew says. "The pictures were awesome. Lots of body paint and big boobs."

"Boobs!" Dustin says. I glare at my brother. I can tell by how well the word is formed that this is not the first time Dustin's heard it. The village that's raising my child is not always as mature as it might be.

Everybody's talking over each other. Chase's sons are on their phones, Googling everyone and everything they can think of to try to figure out who the house might belong to and which of the Keys it might be located in.

No one comments on the fact that the high-profile individual, whoever he or she might be, has been chosen because *Do Over* needs a major ratings boost to survive.

"Has anyone else noticed that we're going to be on another barrier island in the middle of hurricane season?" Deirdre asks.

"We've all noticed." Avery starts to roll her eyes then remembers she's on-camera. "I have a feeling they're not going to be happy until they get footage of us clinging to a rooftop waiting for someone to rescue us."

"I guess Hurricane Charlene wasn't enough for them," Mom says. Charlene was the hurricane that roared up the Gulf Coast, right past Bella Flora, just after we finished renovating her, causing us to spend the night cowering in a Tampa motel bathtub. Last summer, when we were in South Beach, the disaster we faced was entirely man-made.

I see Troy smiling and I can't really blame him. We're all so excited that we barely notice that he's here recording all of our warts and foibles for playback at a future date.

Dustin slides down off my lap and races over to the tree, where my father picks him up and helps him choose a candy cane off a branch. I wish I could forget that he and my mother are no longer the single entity I've always considered them. I'm a mother now myself, and the idea of being a child of divorce at the ripe old age of twenty-four is ridiculous, but it still makes my stomach hurt. The thought of Tonja Kay taking her anger at me out on Bella Flora makes the ache even worse.

I hear the loud whine of a boat motor out in the pass.

An explosion of flashes lights the sky just long enough for someone to get an exterior shot of Bella Flora with a hint of us inside. I wish I were wearing my burqa right now. Or even the big hair and strap-on boobs that I wore in Nashville. I'm going to have to come up with a lighter, more breathable disguise, something that's water-repellent, before we head down to the Keys.

I can feel Troy zooming in on my face. He pans the camera lens slowly across the couch, carefully pausing on each of us briefly before moving on. Unlike his lens, my thoughts move in quick jerks and starts. My mother says it's all about accepting change and moving forward. But I think that's easier for the person making the change than it is for the people who are forced to accept it.

I try to imagine who the "high-profile" individual in the Keys might be, but of course *high-profile* could mean about as much as *celebrity* does. The house we'll be renovating could belong to the president of the United States. Or a *Project Runway* all-star.

Dustin runs to me and climbs into my lap and I hold him tight against me. I don't have to look to know what Troy is shooting. We are the tabloid version of the *Madonna and Child*, but our powers are confined to selling magazines and, maybe, if we're lucky, a successful network television show.

I look around me and I'm reminded that Dustin and I are not alone. We're all bound up with each other and with *Do Over*. And another chance to "do over" our own lives. We've had two shots at this, and we've all made progress. I know I'm not the only one who's hoping that the saying is true. That the third time, somewhere down in the Florida Keys, will be the charm.

A BELLA FLORA CHRISTMAS

This story takes place between
the novels *One Good Thing* and
Best Beach Ever.

Chapter One

Celebrating Christmas with real-life celebrities can be complicated. This is partly because of the paparazzi they attract and partly because of the oversized personalities they possess. No matter how many times we look at their photos splashed across a tabloid cover and tell ourselves that famous people put their pants on one leg at a time just like we do, the truth is they probably don't.

My name is Kyra Singer, and I know all this because I became famous—make that notorious—for falling in love with a movie star named Daniel Deranian while I was working on my first feature film, believing him when he said he loved me, and giving birth to his child. And because my mother, Madeline, is dating a rock star. Yes, my mother. Who I'm pretty sure is one of a very small subset of 52-year-old grandmothers who can claim this distinction. (More on this later.)

It's only a matter of days until Christmas and I'm standing in front of Bella Flora, the seriously cool 1920s Mediterranean Revival–style home perched on the southernmost tip of Pass-a-Grille, a historic fishing village on the west coast of Florida. I don't know where you're spending the holidays, but it's a sunny seventy degrees here and the sky is a brilliant blue streaked with eyebrow-thin white clouds. The streetlights are garland-wrapped with great big red bows tied at the top. Blow-up Santas and palm tree trunks wrapped in Christmas lights line the two small roads that lead on and off the barrier island. There's a much better chance of toasting marshmallows at a bonfire on the beach than in a fireplace. Anyone who's looking for a white Christmas should stay where they are.

Personally, I'll take fine white sand squishing between my toes over snowflakes falling on my head any day—not that I'm an expert, seeing as how I was raised in Atlanta where even the mention of snow empties grocery shelves and causes embarrassing events like 2014's Snowmageddon.

The first time we saw Bella Flora, which was all my mother and co-owners Nicole Grant and Avery Lawford had left in the wake of Malcolm Dyer's Ponzi scheme, she looked like a once-grand dame in serious need of reconstructive surgery and smelled like a locker room. We brought her back to life out of sheer desperation and she did the same for us.

In the afternoon sunlight Bella Flora looks like a wedding cake fresh from the bakery box. Its pale pink walls and acres of windows are trimmed in white icing and accented by bell towers and wrought-iron balconies. The whole confection is topped by a multi-angled barrel-tile roof.

I step through the low wall that encloses a front garden filled with original plants from the twenties and feel the warm glow of love for this home that has been our one safe haven. As I follow a bricked path past a Deco era dolphin fountain, take the rounded steps up to the colonnade, and let myself in the wooden double doors, that glow is dimmed by the knowledge that I've put Bella Flora at risk and could actually lose her.

In the foyer I pause as the house wraps its arms

around me in welcome. Then I follow the sound of my four-year-old son's laughter down the central hallway past the formal living and dining rooms and the Casbah Lounge, which is an ode to Spanish tile, leaded glass, and Moroccan leather, and into the kitchen where he and my mother are making Christmas cookies. Dustin's standing on a chair next to her just like my younger brother Andrew and I used to, pressing holiday-shaped cookie cutters into the dough then transferring them onto the cookie sheet.

His dark eyes are intent on what he's doing, and based on the amount of green and red icing smeared in his dark curls and across the smooth golden cheeks and chin that he inherited from his father, they've been at this for a while. He looks up at me through long dark lashes that any woman would covet and flashes his sunniest smile, also an exact duplicate of his dad's. Except Dustin's is not calculated while his father can flash it—and pretty much any other emotion—on cue. Sometimes I have to remind myself just what Daniel Deranian does for a living and how very good he is at it.

Because of my all-too-public pregnancy and the fact that I gave birth to Daniel's only biological son, at the ripe old age of twenty-seven I've had way more than my fifteen minutes of fame. Dustin has had a whole life full. What began as me signing papers promising to keep Dustin's paternity secret—a feat that proved impossible—has evolved into Daniel's open involvement in Dustin's life, his insistence that Dustin bear his last name, and his more recent demand that Dustin play his son in his upcoming directorial debut. I'm glad that Dustin has a relationship with his father and extremely grateful to him for buying Bella Flora for Dustin and me when we were forced to sell it. I'm less happy with the idea of Dustin portraying Daniel and his real life movie star wife Tonja Kay's son, and there's no more time for hedging. They've already pushed filming back twice. I have to commit or refuse before New Year's.

"Look, Mommy. I cutted out a Santa Cause. And a helf." He holds up the now-smooshed shapes in both hands, beaming.

"Here. There's room for them right there on the baking sheet." My mother shows him where to place them, her smile as warm as her tone is gentle. Mom's always known how to make the most of a holiday without going all Martha Stewart in the process. She's also created a "home" everywhere we filmed *Do Over*, the renovation-turned-reality TV show that took us from

Bella Flora to South Beach, to a private island in the Keys that belonged to a then-reclusive down-on-his-luck rock star named William Hightower, and back again.

I staked everything we had, including Bella Flora, to remodel the Sunshine Hotel, a moldering mid-century hotel just up the beach, in an attempt to take back control of *Do Over*, and lost. We also lost the non-compete lawsuit the network slapped us with. Which has left my mother and me glaringly unemployed and virtually penniless.

This is why I've agreed to rent Bella Flora to a mystery tenant for an amount that gives me the option of turning down the million dollars Daniel and his wife offered for Dustin to play their son.

A text dings in. The knot of panic tightens when I recognize Daniel's phone number. *Coming in the day after tomorrow to bring Dustin's gift. Will text when I land.* There's no asking if that's convenient or mention of the decision I have to make, but I know better than to think the subject won't come up. He and Tonja are not only starring in *The Exchange*, they're investors. And they need Dustin for a lot of reasons, one of them being the publicity value of father and son playing themselves while Daniel's real-life wife plays his mother.

"Kyra?" I look up into my mother's face and see her concern for me. "Everything all right?"

"Absolutely." I can't face another conversation about Daniel's movie or the fact that our son wants to act with his father. And no matter how stressful everything feels at the moment, I don't want to ruin the holiday for Dustin or anyone else. If I don't find a way to pay off the entire loan I took out, it could be the last one we get to spend in Bella Flora.

I watch my mother help Dustin start filling a second cookie sheet and think about how completely I took my childhood and my mother for granted. When our world fell apart, I was shocked to discover how strong she was. I think she and my father were surprised, too. They ended up divorced because he never figured out how to deal with it.

"I'm making these for Billium." Dustin smashes another dough elf onto the baking pan enthusiastically. "'Cuz he's going to be here in a cuppa days. To see Geema."

My mother's cheeks turn red at the mention of William Hightower. It seems that we Singer women have a hard time resisting charismatic personalities. In my case the grand prize was Dustin. In my mother's, well, like I said, it's not every woman her age who gets to sleep with someone as hot as the man formerly known as William the Wild. She has a valid reason to blush.

"Thomas is coming with him," my mother says, referring to Will's thirty-year-old son. "I thought he and Andrew could share the pool house."

I nod and step up behind Dustin to help him with a tricky bit of dough. I know that my mother has been a great influence on Will and he, well, there's a lot more to William than his looks and talent. For one thing he had the good sense to appreciate my mother; something my father had forgotten how to do. Watching her reimagine and rebuild her life out of the ashes of disaster has been completely inspiring. I hope I can be even half the woman she is by the time I turn fifty.

Chapter Two

In late December sunset is an Early Bird Special. At five P.M. I lie in a chaise near the pool watching Dustin play in the Bella Flora replica his father sent him a few Christmases ago and the sky is already beginning to fade. As my son pretends to build a set of bookcases in the playhouse's salon, I wonder if the anonymous renter is an individual or a couple. Or whether there'll be a whole family moving in.

I hate the idea of strangers living here even temporarily, but I guess renting her out is a whole lot better than losing her completely. Still, the anonymity thing makes me uncomfortable. In my experience it's only celebrities and the ultra-wealthy who have reason to hide their identity.

When my cell phone rings I see the Los Angeles area code. It's not Daniel's and I freeze for just a minute before I recognize the phone number.

"Kyra?" Sydney Ryan has two first names and both of them are masculine, which is a testament to how much her father wanted a son and not what she looks or sounds like. She has a face and body that can—and have—stopped traffic, coupled with a husky voice that most men wouldn't dream of trying to resist. Those men are rarely prepared for the tomboy who lives inside the uber feminine package—did I mention how much her father wanted a son?—and are shocked that she understands and cares about what's happening on the football field or baseball diamond. Or that she knows exactly why the hockey players are beating each other to a pulp on the ice and who will likely win. You definitely don't want to go up against her in a speed round of sports trivia.

"Hey, Syd. How are you?"

"I've been better."

This admission is your average person's shriek for help.

"What's wrong?"

"Nothing really."

"Okay."

Sydney is famous for playing female cop Cassie Everheart on a long-running detective show called *Murder 101*. We met five and a half years ago on the set of *Halfway Home* where she was playing her first film role and I was the lowly production assistant who was stupid enough to fall for the leading man. Before Tonja went on the warpath—I wasn't Daniel Deranian's first or last extramarital fling—I wouldn't have said Sydney and I had a ton in common other than growing up in the suburbs of Atlanta. But when the shit started hitting the fan and I became a cliché and pariah, Sydney was the only person on that set who didn't ditch me. Something Tonja Kay did not appreciate. Syd and I have been friends ever since. She's one of those friends that you don't see for a year and then pick up right where you left off. Plus she's one of Dustin's godmothers.

"Something's off on the set. I'm not sure what, but I was on my way to FedEx Dustin's present. And then I thought about how long it's been since I've seen you guys."

She doesn't mention Jake Bodie, her co-star and real-life boyfriend, and I don't ask. Given the things that have been written about me, I will be the very last person on the planet to bring up the shots of him with a young starlet that I saw on the front page of a tabloid during my last trip to the grocery store.

"I'd kind of like to get out of town for the holiday. If you have room." The last is offered in a timid tone that's decidedly un-Sydney-like.

"There's always room for you, Syd. But I just want to make sure you remember that Pass-a-Grille is only about two and a half miles long and two blocks wide." Sydney swore off small towns, cities, and suburbs years ago, including her own.

"I'm not coming for the square footage," she says. "I'm coming for the company."

In my head, I start moving the company we're already expecting around. Bella Flora is a big house, but she's going to be bulging with people. Sydney could have Dustin's room. Or even bunk in with me. Plus the cottage at the Sunshine Hotel that my mother is taking is mostly ready.

"Great." I get up and walk over to the playhouse where Dustin is putting his tools into his tool belt. "When will you be coming in?"

"Christmas Eve day. The day after tomorrow."

There's a brief silence as I register the fact that she knew she was coming before she called. It's the same day William and Thomas Hightower and Daniel are arriving.

"Perfect," I say. Now there will be three celebrities at Bella Flora. Which makes our chances of getting through Christmas without a visitation from the paparazzi less than zero.

"Text me the details. Dustin and I will pick you up at the airport."

Friends don't let friends spend the holidays alone.

. . .

I've just hung up when the doorbell rings. Through the open windows I hear my mother answering the front door. There are greetings and exclamations—I have no doubt hugs and kisses are exchanged. By the time we get inside, Nicole Grant (I still can't think of her as a Giraldi even though she and special agent Joe Giraldi are now married and the parents of eight and a half month old twin girls), Avery Lawford, architect and newly licensed contractor who spearheaded the renos we did for *Do Over*, and Bitsy Baynard, who was an heiress and sponsor before her husband ran off with an exotic dancer and everything Bitsy owned, are talking a mile a minute. As you can see, a lot of us aren't what we used to be. Some of us are more.

A happy *woof* snags Dustin's attention. "Cherlock is here!" he shouts as we head into the kitchen. He breaks into a huge smile when he spots the French bulldog that is all Bitsy's husband left behind when he disappeared with her fortune.

There's a knock on the kitchen door and my brother Andrew, whom I can no longer refer to as my "little" brother since he's now a college graduate and well over six feet tall, steps inside. Dustin is in double heaven. "You ready, little man?" My brother hugs our mother, scratches Sherlock behind one bat-wing ear, and scoops up his nephew. "Geedad's outside. We're going to have a guys' night out and a great big manly pizza."

They're gone in a flash and we carry snacks and drinks out to the loggia and settle around the wrought-iron table to watch and toast the sunset. Nikki, Joe, and the girls are just back from Miami, and my mother was visiting William Hightower down on Mermaid Point, so it's been a while since we've all been together. Avery reaches for a Cheez Doodle, which is her go-to snack.

To my knowledge, Avery's never met a cheese product that she doesn't like.

My mother has brought out toasted Bagel Bites and little hot dogs wrapped in dough. Bitsy spreads Ted Peters smoked fish spread on a cracker while Nikki pours wine into glasses. "God, I missed you guys. And this." She raises her glass and waves it under her nose. "I've officially stopped nursing. I've got a lot of toasts and drinks to catch up on."

"You look great." My mother's always the first to offer a compliment.

"Well, I'm still standing." Nikki's tall with great cheekbones and auburn hair that she's wearing in a messy bun at the nape of her neck. Her eyes are a stunning green. She's forty-eight, but there's a glow about her that's new. "Though sometimes I reach the end of the day and it's all a blur and I know I've been operating on automatic pilot."

"Where are Sofia and Gemma?"

"Joe offered to feed them and get them down for the night," Nikki says. "I pretty much ran out of the cottage before he could change his mind."

"He's a good guy." Avery sounds a bit wistful. She

and her longtime boyfriend Chase Hardin are no longer living together, but they do seem to be dating.

"He is," Nikki agrees. "Even if he's still making me look like a slug in the parenting department."

"When do the Giraldis get in?" my mother asks.

"Day after tomorrow."

Joe's parents and grandmother Nonna Sofia—who's still claiming credit for Nikki's pregnancy due to an ancient Italian curse gone amok—stay next door at the Cottage Inn. But our Inn is going to be stuffed to the brim, too. We're lucky to have a pool house if not a manger. I start moving guests and extra beds around in my head.

Sherlock is stretched out under Bitsy's chair. He snuffles occasionally and rouses slightly when the Bagel Bites and mini hot dogs get close. We drink and nibble as the sun slips toward the water, dappling the surface with pinpricks of light.

Finally, Maddie asks, "Who has a good thing to share?"

There are a few groans, but none of us are surprised. My mother began the tradition of coming up with one good thing each sunset back when we were all completely broke and desperately renovating Bella Flora.

Then, coming up with anything good was a serious challenge.

"You first, Maddie," Avery says while the rest of us sip our wine and reach for snacks.

"All right." She places her wineglass on the table and settles in her chair. "It's really good to have everyone together again. And both of my children and my grandson here for the holidays."

We drink to this and I watch Avery lick the Cheez Doodle residue from her fingers.

"You're having regular carnal knowledge of a rock star and that's the best you can do?" Nikki teases.

"No," my mother says. "But that's the best I'm *going* to do."

Nikki laughs at my mother's telltale blush. "Ahhh, that's a different thing altogether. You are an inspiration, Madeline Singer. Maybe you should write a book about how to have a knock-your-socks-off romance after fifty." Nikki was once a dating guru and A-list matchmaker with offices on both coasts and a bestseller of her own. Before her brother's Ponzi scheme brought her career and her company Heart Inc. to a screeching halt.

"Right. And maybe you can write the chapter on

giving birth just shy of it," Avery says to Nikki. "Special agent Joe Giraldi isn't exactly chopped liver."

There's laughter. The easy kind that comes from knowing people through bad times as well as good.

"True. But we're both too exhausted most of the time to do anything about it." Nikki yawns.

"We're still waiting for your good thing," Bitsy points out.

"Okay." Nikki takes another sip of wine. "I'm still nowhere near as good as Joe in the parenting department, but I'm improving. My one good thing is that I'm starting to believe that it is possible to teach an old dog new tricks."

Sherlock snuffles in his sleep and we share another round of smiles. My mother's gaze turns to Bitsy. "Anything good to report on Bertrand's whereabouts?"

Bitsy sighs. She's sworn to track her husband and her fortune down then haul them back and is working part-time for an attorney in Tampa who specializes in those things in trade for her help. Bertie not only stole everything, he left without divorcing her. Which has to make you wonder whether he thinks there's some way on God's earth that Bitsy would ever take him back.

"There was a sighting in Montenegro, which has a

plethora of banks and a no extradition policy. That's as close to a good thing as I'm getting tonight." Bitsy raises her glass and drains it, which doesn't mean much since she's drunk us all under the table on plenty of occasions. "But honestly at this point he could be anywhere."

We think about that for a few minutes as the reddish-golden ball of sun hovers above the Gulf preparing for splashdown.

"How about you, Avery?" My mother asks, pulling her sweater around her as the breeze picks up and the temperature begins to drop.

"Well, I've got your Sunshine cottage pretty much completed, and I'm going to advertise my design-and-build services in a tiny house publication to see what kind of interest I can stir up. So, my good thing is what I hope will be a new beginning in the new year." Avery raises her glass and we clink all around. We all thought she'd rejoin Chase in the construction company their fathers built, but apparently their relationship issues aren't just personal. We drink and pour a last glass. I'm feeling the alcohol but not quite enough to share a good thing and mean it. Instead of buoying me, each good thing I've heard tonight has made me feel even more wretched.

My mother looks at me and raises an eyebrow. "Kyra?"

The truth is that spending six to eight weeks on a movie set with my son's father, his vindictive wife, and their family may be more than I can bear. Not even for the money that will help us hold onto Bella Flora or to let Dustin be a part of his father's directorial debut. I drop my eyes, ashamed of my wussiness and weighed down by the guilt I feel for risking the home Daniel gave Dustin and me that means so much to all of us. Somehow I've become a "waffler," continually considering the pros and cons, but unable to reach a decision that I can live with. Which is extremely unlike me. Normally my decisions are made by my gut, not my brain. And they occur at the speed of light.

"Sorry." I scrape back my chair and stand. "I'm going to have to take a pass tonight. I—I have to finish editing some video before Dustin gets back." I swallow, nearly choking on the lie. "I'll try to come up with two good things next sunset." I still don't meet my mother's eyes as I turn and flee.

Chapter Three

The first of the paparazzi makes an appearance Christmas Eve morning and my first thought is that certain celebrities' public relations' people do not shut down for the holidays.

"Hello, luv! G'morning Dustin!" Nigel Bracken is tall, pale, and British, and I've come to know his face and voice almost as well as my own. He's wearing one of his ill-fitting Hawaiian shirts and a pith helmet to protect his sparsely covered head from the sun. He stands on a spot just beyond the property line that he's made his own, as if he had a reserved parking space. I don't answer or smile as I wheel Dustin's jogging stroller out of the garage. Dustin's getting a bit big for the stroller, but it's the only way I can take him with me and jog any distance. Plus it has storage for his sand toys, which are an important part of any beach outing.

I used to wear disguises and prided myself on evading or fooling the paparazzi, but it takes a huge amount of time and effort and in the end these bottom-feeders know where we live, what cars we drive, and even what grocery stores and restaurants we frequent.

"Aww, come on, luv! It's practically Christmas!" He says when he's unable to get a clean shot. I remain silent and attempt to keep my face expressionless, but not bitchy, which isn't as easy as it sounds. My neutral look comes off as royally pissed in tabloid photos. I suspect there is some special paparazzi face-correcting or mood-modulating lens that can turn carefully impassive into an ugly sneer. You know, like an Instagram filter, only instead of Crema through Perpetua they've got a full range from Mildly Disgruntled to Bitch from Hell.

My son, who is far friendlier and more generous than I am, flashes one of his gap-toothed smiles at the photographer.

"What time do the Hightowers arrive?" Nigel shouts

as he shoots. "Is Sydney Ryan's boyfriend going to show up? Or has he already ditched her?"

I wonder how he even knew the Hightowers and Sydney were coming and how much he already knows about her relationship with Jake Bodie, but I remain silent. If Nigel's going to continue to make money stalking us, he's going to have to do his own damn research. I am not my paparazzi's keeper. "Will Daniel be coming into town?"

"My Dandiel!" Dustin's smile gets bigger, and I pray that Nigel is only fishing for answers and not about to ruin the big fish's surprise. I take a few minutes to stretch, careful to block his money shot of Dustin while attempting to keep moving so he can't focus on my butt.

"Come on, Kyra! It's almost Christmas!" He says this as if we're friends and not prey and hunter. The fact that he considers us to be on a first-name basis makes my stomach turn. "Just one clean shot of the two of you and I'm out of here."

This is a lie that I've fallen for before. At one point we tried offering a daily photo opportunity while keeping things boring so they'd give up and go away. But boring only works if there's bigger game in town, and given our holiday guest list, I don't think that's going to happen. Unless we figure out how to fake a Kardashian sighting. Or spend the entire holiday sitting around staring at our navels. Even then they'd probably want to document it.

Still silent, I jog slowly down the driveway then cut to the right so that I can jog along the bay. Nigel doesn't follow, and I try to enjoy the warmth of the sun on my face and arms and the soft breeze off the water. A whiff of fish reaches my nostrils at the historic Merry Pier and I turn west onto Eighth Avenue, which serves as Pass-a-Grille's "main street." Like all of the avenues that stretch between the bay and the gulf, it's exactly one block wide.

• • •

The architecture is Deco. The concrete buildings are painted in bright tropical colors. They house a few small galleries, boutiques, and restaurants along with a well-known jewelry store owned by a former hippie. A photographer I don't recognize steps off the sidewalk in front of a biker bar called Shadrack's that's been there since the motorcycle was invented. "When do you and Dustin leave for location?" he shouts. "Tonja Kay says she has a very close relationship with your son and that it's you who's the problem!"

I grit my teeth to keep myself from responding. Tonja Kay hasn't been allowed anywhere near my son since she showered profanity all over the two of us then tried to take him away from me.

I reach The Hurricane Seafood Restaurant, which sits on a prime corner across from the beach. Personally, I think naming a restaurant perched at sea level near the tip of a barrier island "The Hurricane" is asking for trouble, but over the decades it's mushroomed from a rambling concrete shanty into a multi-tiered Victorian-style building that might have been transported from New England.

Someone calls my name and I look up to see yet another paparazzo lying in wait like a third tag team member. Bill has a potato-shaped nose and a face that's even pastier than Nigel's. That's what comes of hiding under rocks waiting for your prey. His camera drive is firing, but I don't break my stride as I maneuver the jogging stroller down to firm sand and head north.

My breathing evens out as we pass the Sunshine Hotel and then the Don CeSar, the huge pink castle of a hotel that was built right around the same time as

Bella Flora. I don't bother to look behind me because these paparazzi aren't into running or working out. The only things they "lift" are alcoholic beverages. I slow behind an old hotel on Gulf Boulevard across from the neighborhood where my father now lives. Dustin clambers out of the stroller and retrieves his mesh bag of sand toys, which he carries down to the hard-packed sand near the waters' edge. Within minutes he's hunkered down happily filling a first bucket with wet sand. I kneel down next to him.

In about an hour or so my brother will pick us up in the hotel parking lot so that we can shower and dress and grab some lunch at my dad's place. Afterward, I'll take Andrew's car to the airport to pick up Sydney. I hate having to put all this time and energy into avoiding people whose sole mission in life is to harass us, but like I said, it's not my job to make the paps' job easier and there's no reason to call attention to ourselves. My brother's car is about as nondescript as you can get and our mission is to blend in. Or at least to not stand out.

• • •

We wait in the cell phone lot at Tampa International Airport for about fifteen minutes—this is a very civilized invention and any airport that doesn't have one totally should. When we pull up outside baggage claim, I'm glad I didn't waste any energy on a disguise, because Sydney is not trying to blend into the crowd in any way. But then she's never been one to "hide her light under a bushel." Not that there's room for anything, including a sliver of light, under the skintight clothes she has on.

I work my way up to the curb, put on the parking brake, and walk around to open the trunk as several photographers aim cameras and shout questions at Sydney. The best thing about Andrew's ancient Mustang is how darkly tinted the windows are. Even I can't see Dustin through them, and I know exactly where he's sitting.

Sydney spots me and walks over, ignoring the photographers. When she throws her arms around me, I feel her sinewy strength. I'm in pretty good shape from jogging and running after a four-year-old, but Sydney's workout regimen has always been brutal. Her face and body are important assets to her career—there are no leading lady detectives with back fat on prime-time television—and Sydney has never aspired to comedy. Plus she was that girl who played on the boys' baseball, basketball, and football teams in high school. There was no hurdle Sydney refused to jump to please her father.

Despite the five-hour plane trip, she looks like she's just stepped out of hair and makeup. Although she looks like a "high maintenance" type, she only has one carry-on. A gaily wrapped Christmas present pokes out of her handbag. If she ever decided to walk away from acting, she could totally start a consulting business on packing light.

"Can you give us a smile?" One photographer shouts at us.

"Are you upset that Jake is in Vail with another woman?" The other adds.

Sydney's smile falters and I see a flash of surprise in her eyes, but she says nothing as she stows her carry-on in the trunk then lets herself into the passenger seat. She slumps slightly as soon as the door clicks closed, but by the time I start the car and begin edging away from the curb, she's turning in her seat and grinning at Dustin. "Hello my gorgeous man," she says. "You are looking *very* grown up."

This gets a huge smile and giggle from my son. Sydney puts her fingers to her lips and blows him a kiss. He pretends to catch it then makes a big kissing sound against his fist and flings one back. They've been doing this routine since he was a baby. Sydney has a real way with children.

"Is almost Chritsmas!" Dustin proclaims happily. "I get to open a present tonight!" He looks at her through his lashes. "Did you bring me a present?"

"Dustin!" I try to catch his eye in the rearview mirror.

"Jus wondrin," he says innocently.

"Of course I did," Sydney says. "And I bet you'll get presents from Santa Claus, too."

Dustin nods and his smile gets bigger. This is undoubtedly true. With all the friends and family sharing Christmas this year, Dustin will be buried in gifts and he'll be thrilled with every one of them.

Sydney turns around and tightens her seatbelt as we leave the airport behind us. Dustin yawns and settles into his car seat. We're barely halfway across the Howard Frankland Bridge when Dustin's head starts to nod.

"Are your parents upset that you're not going home for Christmas?" I ask Sydney tentatively.

"No. The whole family was going on a cruise and I

had already passed." She hesitates briefly. "I was supposed to spend the holiday with Jake in Vail. But that sort of fell apart. Apparently he didn't want to waste the reservations." Her jaw hardens as she turns her gaze out the window, and I do not ask who he's in Vail with. Sydney's rarely at a loss for words. She'll tell me what's going on when she's ready.

When we arrive at Bella Flora, I carry Dustin, who's sound asleep and a dead weight in my arms, into the house. My mother hugs Sydney hello then begins to flutter around. "Will and Thomas will be here within the hour," she says happily. "I've gone ahead and moved into the master. Are you sure that's what you want?"

"Yep," I reply easily, having thought this through from lots of angles. "That way you guys will have some privacy and Syd and I can share a room and still each have our own bed." Sydney and I have been known to sit up talking most of the night and it's been a while. We have a lot to catch up on.

"Positive?" My mother asks.

"One hundred percent," I say even though it is a little weird that my mother has a romantic relationship and I don't.

"I could use you in the kitchen once Dustin's down

for a nap and Sydney's settled," she says. "I need an eggnog taster and someone to help wrap a few last-minute gifts."

"Be right down," I say as we start up the stairs. On the landing I point Sydney toward the bedroom we're going to be sharing then carry Dustin into his room, where I slip him gently into his car bed and pull his door closed behind me.

Chapter Four

It's a good thing Bella Flora has so many thousands of square feet, because we're planning to pack a lot of people inside her tonight and we'll have even more people here tomorrow for Christmas.

It turns dark and rainy around four. By five o'clock we've got the Casbah Lounge all decked out. A large punch bowl of spiked eggnog sits on the bar and each tile-topped table has small bowls of spiced nuts and Chex Mix and its own candle. The Casbah has leaded glass windows, red leather banquettes, and a riot of Moorish tile that covers everything from the floor to the bar to the arched pillars and posts. Whenever I'm in here I picture

Bogie toasting Bacall while "As Time Goes By" plays softly in the background.

The unspiked eggnog has been relegated to the salon along with more nibbles and finger foods. The main event will take place tomorrow. A fire has been lit in the fireplace and the tree, now completely decorated, stands in front of one of the floor-to-ceiling windows that overlook the pool and the pass. The star at the top of the tree is the one Andrew and I grew up with, and the ornaments we made in kindergarten and elementary school share pride of place with tinsel and colored lights. Dustin's ornaments, which include a small fire truck and a palm tree that says Pass-a-Grille on it, hang wherever he could reach. Garlands and strings of popcorn encircle the tree and candy canes and chocolate Santas dangle from the tips of the lower branches.

Dustin shrieks with glee when Bitsy Baynard arrives with Sherlock—who has a large red bow tied around his neck. He follows Dustin back to the salon and settles on the floor at his feet, his chin on his front paws. Avery's right behind them, and I assume she rushed here after working on one of the Sunshine cottages, because there are still small globs of paint in her blond hair.

"Where are Nikki and Joe and the girls?" she asks

as she pinches a Cheez Doodle from a bowl and ladles herself a cup of eggnog. "Their cottage was dark when we left. I figured they were already here."

"They were supposed to be, but Joe's parents and Nonna Sofia had car trouble on the way down . . . they went to pick them up in Gainesville." My mother hands her a holiday napkin. If a snack doesn't turn her fingers orange, Avery isn't interested. "They'll all be here tomorrow along with the Franklins and the Hardins."

Maddie is in perpetual motion, refilling trays, making sure the eggnog keeps flowing, making everyone feel welcome. When she pauses it's next to William Hightower whose dark hair is threaded with gray and whose high cheekbones and hatchet nose attest to his Native American forbearers even though he insists he has far more Florida Cracker blood running through his veins than Seminole. His dark eyes follow Maddie wherever she goes and a small smile plays at the corner of his lips. The laps he began swimming every day during his last and final stint in rehab have left him lean and chiseled. Hours fishing out on the flats that dot the Florida Keys have left his face burnished by the sun.

My father frowns slightly when my mother comes in or out of Will's orbit, but I'm all out of sympathy.

He's the one who screwed up. And he was the first one to date even before they announced their plans to divorce. But living with the ramifications of his own actions is not my father's strong suit. I'm relieved that he's moved out of Bella Flora and is finally attempting to get on with his life. I love him, but seriously, it's way past time.

Thomas Hightower steps through the French doors, his dark hair slick with rain. He's a less rugged and weathered version of his rock star father. Because of, or in spite of, his turbulent childhood, he skipped the drug scene his father once wallowed in and prefers numbers to music. He may not be the player his father once was, but that doesn't mean he hasn't noticed Sydney. I mean, who doesn't? Even my not-so-little-brother Andrew lights up like the Christmas tree when she smiles or speaks to him.

"Are you ready to light Max's menorah?"

"Max Nemorah!" Dustin beams as I pull out the menorah and set it on the mantel.

Hanukkah is over—I never have grasped the Jewish calendar—but we light all eight candles each year to honor Max Golden, who owned the Nautical Art Deco home that we renovated for the first full season of *Do*

Over. The candle holders are shaped like comedy masks because Max and his wife Millie were once the George Burns and Gracie Allen of Miami Beach. We talk about Max often. I don't want any of us to ever forget that he saved my son's life.

The others gather around us. Dustin repeats the prayer with me as I light the candles—we've both memorized it phonetically. It's amazing what you can learn how to do on YouTube.

Large quantities of eggnog are consumed. Our collective mood mellows. The mix of Christmas carols is random and eclectic—I'm not sure who curated the playlist—but it includes everything from Johnny Cash's "I'll Be Home for Christmas" to Alvin and the Chipmunks' "Christmas Don't Be Late." We're listening to Bing Crosby's "White Christmas" and settling in around the tree to watch Dustin open a present when the doorbell rings.

"Maybe it's Santa Cause!" Dustin jumps up, grabs my hand and drags me to the front door, Sherlock on our heels. When I open it, it *is* Santa Claus. A tall, perfectly turned-out version complete with red apple cheeks, white beard and mustache, a stomach straining against a red velvet suit, and matching fur-trimmed cap. I look past him half expecting to see a sleigh hitched to the curb. Instead I see a stretch limo idling in front of the garden wall. Nigel and his passel of paparazzi cohorts are standing near it.

"It's Santa Cause!" Dustin shouts. Sherlock woofs happily.

In a deep voice that makes his padded stomach go up and down, Santa shouts, "Ho! Ho! Ho! Young man! Merrrrrry Christmas!"

Normally, Dustin is the first to recognize his father through any disguise, but it's Christmas Eve and despite the department store and Salvation Army Santas, he hasn't yet begun to question whether or not Santa Claus exists. Beyond excited, he throws his arms around Santa's waist and shouts "Merry Christmas!" right back.

"You were supposed to text when you were on your way," I whisper just before Santa lifts Dustin up and whirls him around, sending Nigel, Bill, and the other photographers into a shooting frenzy that lights up the darkness.

"Sorry. Didn't get the chance." He covers this with another "Ho! Ho! Ho!" while Dustin squeals happily and Sherlock gives another woof and wags his tail.

"Are you deriviring presents?" Dustin remembers Santa's actual function as Daniel sets him back on his feet.

"I have one for a Mister Dustin Deranian. His father asked me to deliver it."

"I'm Dustin Deranium." Dustin is quivering with excitement. "What did my Dandiel send me?"

"I've got it right here," Santa says cheerily as he reaches into the shadowed area just beyond the door and comes back with a large wrapped box. "May I come in?"

Dustin looks up at me his mouth an O of surprise. He didn't think twice about Santa ringing the doorbell to hand deliver a gift, but it apparently strikes him as strange that Santa not only wants to come inside, but has to ask me for permission.

"Of course," I say, not wanting to be the one to ruin the moment. "Maybe you can go ask Geema to wrap up the Christmas cookies you made for Santa so that he can take them with him."

"Want my present first." His chin juts out and I see the determined look I'm learning to recognize settle on his face. He flew past the terrible twos without the slightest eruption, and his threes were pretty mellow, but lately he's become less malleable and more unpredictable.

"Dustin . . ."

"No problem, Ma'am," Santa chuckles. He places the box on the floor of the foyer. "He can open it right now."

Dustin grins in triumph and immediately squats down in front of the box. I move to close the door but Daniel steps slightly to his right so I can't reach it. Santa's eyes twinkle. Daniel is clearly excited about this gift and is already anticipating Dustin's reaction to it. I'm just relieved it's not another replica of Bella Flora or something else too big to deal with. Sherlock sniffs the box aggressively then looks up at us and whimpers.

"Lift off the top, Dustin," Santa urges as he moves even further to his right.

The lid comes off and I hear another whimper. But it's not Sherlock or Dustin who makes the sound. It's. . .

"It's a puppy! My Dandiel gave me a puppy!" Dustin lifts the squirming, wriggling, whimpering gift and clutches it in his arms, his face suffused with happiness.

Flashes go off like fireworks and I realize that Dustin

and the puppy are perfectly framed and lit in the doorway. This is not an accident.

My eyes narrow as the puppy licks Dustin's face.
Sherlock doesn't look any happier than I do. This puppy
is all long legs and huge feet. His head is big and square.
"What kind of dog is this?" I demand.

"Great Dane," Daniel says in his Santa voice.
"They're great with children." If he *Ho! Ho! Ho*s right
now, I don't think I'll be responsible for my actions.

"This is not the kind of gift Santa Claus, or anyone
else, should just deliver without checking first," I say
through gritted teeth even though we both know there's
nothing I can do about it. Dustin is holding on to that
puppy like he has no intention of ever letting go. Plus
there's a crowd of photographers outside shooting their
pestilent hearts out. Photos of Daniel/Santa leaving
with a rejected puppy while Dustin sobs would go viral
before I got the front door closed.

Daniel looks at me like he can't wait to see what
happens next. Slamming the door in Santa's face would
be almost as bad as sending him away with the rejected
puppy. Daniel has staged a coup without firing a single shot.

"Dustin, why don't you go show everybody the

puppy and ask Geema to wrap up those cookies for Santa."

Dustin looks up. "Can't Santa stay and bisit?" The puppy squirms in his arms. It's almost as big as he is.

After a quick look at my face, Daniel shakes his head. "Thanks for the invitation, but I have to get back to my deliveries," he says in that hearty Santa voice. "I'll wait right here for those cookies."

Daniel steps inside and closes the front door behind him as Dustin runs back down the central hallway, the puppy crushed to his chest. Sherlock runs after him. I am seething with anger. If I were a cartoon character steam would be pouring out of my ears.

Ignoring my reaction, Daniel wraps his hands around my waist and pulls me close to him. I hold myself stiff, determined to cling to my anger, but underneath the padding and the fake fur I can feel his lithe hardness. He leans his head down and grazes his lips over mine. I do not respond and I'm pretty sure I don't whimper. The fake beard tickles, and I inhale his spicy scent as his hands slip over my rear to bring me closer. The song "I Saw Mommy Kissing Santa Claus" runs through my head, and I order myself to disengage. But myself refuses to obey. A woof from the salon and Dustin's excited voice tell me he's busy showing everyone his new puppy and not on his way back with cookies.

Daniel nuzzles the top of my head with his chin and runs his hands up my back, gentle but knowing.

"No. I'm not doing this again." I say this even as I feel my will weakening like it always does when he applies himself to seducing me.

"Not doing what?" It's a husky murmur I feel more than hear as his lips trail their way down my neck. One hand comes to rest just beneath my breast. My body rouses and clamors for more. In my defense, he is one of the all-time sexiest men alive. Just ask *People* magazine.

"Giving in to you. To this."

His lips linger over the sensitive spot in the hollow of my shoulder then stretch into a smile.

It takes way longer than it should, but I finally detach myself and step back. I draw a deep breath. "Where's Mrs. Claus and the family?"

"North Pole," he says easily.

I give him a look.

He shrugs. "Disney World. We're combining the holiday with some last minute pre-production details." This is where *The Exchange* is supposed to start filming in the middle of January. It's a story about a kidnapping that takes place at the theme park. I still can't believe Disney is allowing itself to be tied even fictionally to a child's abduction, but Daniel Deranian and Tonja Kay may be too big to say no to. Now that Brangelina has broken up, they are *the* Hollywood power couple.

"So what was all this about tonight?" I manage to put another couple of inches between us.

"I've always given Dustin a gift."

"But not in person. Not dressed as Santa. And not with a pack of paparazzi cued up and waiting for your arrival." I watch his face, what I can see of it through the Santa makeup and hair. "And a Great Dane? Really?"

"Bella Flora's big enough for a big dog. And every child should have one."

I've seen the pictures of Daniel and Tonja Kay with their children, their children's individual nannies, and the family dogs traveling all over the world. If you have enough money and staff, nothing is too difficult to manage. We don't even have enough money to hold onto Bella Flora.

"We're moving out of Bella Flora on January second. We have a tenant. I told you I'd find a way to pay off the loan and I have." Once again I try not to think about how I put Bella Flora at risk and why this tenant insists on anonymity.

"For God's sake, Kyra. All you have to do is let Dustin be in the movie and spend the six weeks on location with him and you won't *have* to rent it out."

"I haven't decided about the movie yet," I snap. "And I've already signed a rental agreement."

"We'll use Dustin's salary to pay off the loan up front so that Bella Flora will be free and clear before you're due on set. Plus we'll reimburse the tenant for his deposit. We *need* Dustin to play the part."

"Just like you needed photos of him receiving your adorable gift tonight?"

His lips turn downward into a frown, which is not a good look on Santa. "You're making this way more complicated than it needs to be, Kyra. Dustin wants to be in the movie and we want him to be a part of it." The *we* is instinctive. He and Tonja are one, at least when it comes to business.

"For the publicity."

He doesn't admit this, but he doesn't deny it, either. "Because he's perfect for the role."

"I told you I'm still thinking. The harder you push the harder it is to say yes."

"Don't be crazy." He reaches out a hand to cup my cheek. "There's no need to cut off your nose to spite your face."

"I hate that saying. And I'm not crazy. The only crazy thing I've ever done is fall for you." I reach for his hand and pull it from my face. "I told you I'm thinking. I'll let you know when I reach a decision."

At that moment Dustin runs up to us clutching a paper bag filled with what are undoubtedly crushed Christmas cookies. He hands them to Daniel. "Thank you for the puppy, Santa Cause! Thas exactly what I wanted forever!"

"You're welcome, young man," Daniel says in that gruff yet warm Santa voice. "You be sure and let your father know that I delivered it as promised." He nods down at Dustin, still completely in character. But as he turns to go, I see what look like tears glistening in his eyes.

"I hope you and your mother have a very Merry Christmas, too."

Chapter Five

It's after midnight by the time most of us make it up to bed. I look in on Dustin and see him wrapped up with the puppy and the blankets. I know letting them sleep together from the beginning is undoubtedly a mistake, but it's not like we have a spare dog bed or a crate lying around. Plus it's Christmas Eve and tomorrow—or actually today—is a big day. I don't have the strength to deal with a lonely puppy up crying all night and I don't want to inflict it on others.

I'm way too tired to do more than splash water on my face and brush my teeth, but I do have the energy to give Sydney some shit for the number of tiny plastic containers of cosmetics arranged on the sink—I'm amazed she fit any clothes into that carry-on—and the amount of time she's spent on her "beauty regimen."

"I'm thirty," she says as she massages a second layer of cream onto her face and down her neck. "Which is practically fifty in Hollywood. I'm my only real asset and I'm not a big enough name to let myself go." She applies some sort of conditioner to her hair and then begins to tweeze her eyebrows.

She's wearing a plum-colored satin nightgown trimmed in lace with a matching robe, which is about as far from the ancient boxers and T-shirt I sleep in as it's possible to get. On the outside she looks like an exotic butterfly, on the inside she's more like a squirrel cataloguing its acorns. Not for the first time I'm grateful that I've always worked behind the camera and not in front of it, and that my inside and my outside are in sync.

"Is it weird knowing your mother's having sex down the hall?" she asks, catching my eye in the mirror.

"I'm willing to bet they're already asleep," I say as we share a smile. "But, yeah. I never even thought of her as anything except my mother until my parents got divorced. And if you would have asked me then, I would have said they'd had sex twice—once about nine months before Andrew and I were born. But I'm getting used to it. It's kind of nice to know that fifty's not too late to start a relationship. You know?"

Sydney makes no comment. She's still looking at herself in the mirror, but I can tell she's thinking about something—or someone—else. I'm pretty sure it's not my mother and Will.

"So, what happened with Jake?" I didn't intend to bring this up, but he's apparently in Vail with someone else right now and she's barely mentioned him since she got here. And she's the one who introduced the subject of relationships.

It takes her so long to answer that I think she isn't going to. I'm about to apologize for bringing him up when she says, "I don't know. We had this huge fight after those photos of him and that . . . Andrea . . . surfaced and he stormed out. I'd see him on the set every day, but he just kept acting like I was the one who did something wrong."

"Yeah." I watch her tilt her head to check out every angle. "A lot of guys seem to believe the best defense is a strong offense. I think they teach them that when they start playing sports and they just apply it to everything."

She snorts, but there's a sob in there somewhere. "I didn't know he was still going to Vail. And I sure as hell didn't know he was taking someone else with him." She finally turns away from the mirror. In my room we head for our beds and she says, "I think I'm going to take a nice, long break from men."

It's my turn to snort as I pull back my covers and climb between the sheets. "Really? Because I think Thomas and Andrew both have the hots for you. I'd kind of hate to see my brother get crushed."

"I'll be gentle," she says as she pulls her covers up to her chin. "I'm not trying to start anything." Her voice drops. "I guess I'm just kind of lonely."

Your average person would be shocked to know that a beautiful and well-known actress deals with the same kind of stuff they do. But in the end it all comes down to who we let into our lives and the choices that we make. I sigh and think about Daniel's Santa stunt. I don't like being manipulated, and I especially hate how hard it is to keep my emotional distance from him. It barely took him two weeks to get me in bed and make me fall in love with him during the filming of *Halfway Home*. You'd think I would have built up immunity by now.

Six weeks on a film set with him and his wife and their children? I don't see how I would ever survive it. And how would it make Dustin feel knowing that they all get to live together and be a part of Daniel's life while he gets the occasional visit and over-the-top gift?

"What was all that with the puppy?" Sydney asks as if she's following my disjointed train of thought.

"Well, I know Daniel loves Dustin. And he does like to give him serious gifts. But the timing and the staging? He and Tonja have sunk a lot of their own money into this film and to Daniel's directorial debut. I don't think there's much they wouldn't do to help guarantee its success."

"Including bribing Dustin with a puppy?" she asks with a yawn.

"Dustin already wants to 'hact' with his father so the puppy's probably just an extra inducement. Some of that was for the media. There's not much hard news over the holidays and that was a beautifully orchestrated, pull-at-your-heartstrings kind of moment that's bound to get a lot of attention."

"And if you're not seduced by the money or lulled by the warm, pull-at-your-heartstrings moments?" Sydney asks.

"They'll go back to playing hardball." I've already experienced this on more than one occasion. "You were there the first time Tonja came after me, Syd. Honestly, I deserved to be chucked off that film. I was a complete and total fool for believing Daniel actually loved me. But you—you didn't really have to get involved."

Sydney repositions her covers and sighs. "I always side with the underdog—it's one of my biggest failings. Besides, if I hadn't been in Hollywood as long as I had at that point, it could have been me."

I stop staring at the ceiling to look at her. In the shards of moonlight that filter through the window, I can see her wince. "What do you mean?"

There's a long beat of silence and then she says, "Daniel hit on me when I was reading for the part. He was subtle, but his intention was clear."

I hold my breath and wait for her to go on. Even though I'm pretty sure I don't want to hear this.

"I'd been around long enough to know that's not the best way to get a part or hold on to one. I turned him down as gracefully as I knew how—that's an important skill in my line of work." A wry smile twists her lips. "I don't think he was really all that interested in me.

But if he hadn't set his sights on you so quickly, I might not have skated off so easily."

I try to take in this rewriting of the most important part of my history to date. "And this is the first time you're telling me this?"

She goes up on one elbow. "At the time you were in love and as I recall it, that love was almost completely blind." She swallows. "And we didn't know each other that well. It didn't seem like the right time to bring it up."

"Seriously?" I really can't believe this. All this time I've told myself that Daniel met me and simply couldn't help himself. "You didn't think I should have known that I wasn't his first choice?"

"Oh, Kyra. What makes you think *I* was his first choice? Tonja probably knew he hit on me the same way she knew the first time he kissed you—she makes it her business to know what's happening on Daniel's sets. Besides, what would have been the point? Tonja was already moving to have you thrown off the picture. Then you were pregnant with Dustin. How would knowing that he'd hit on me have been helpful?"

"Jeez!" I flop onto my back and stare up at the shadowed ceiling, still trying to absorb the shock and what feels like a betrayal. Would it have made me more cautious if I'd known he'd wanted Sydney? Would it have made me realize how easily he could transfer his interest from one potential lover to another?

"I'm sorry," Sydney says. "I just couldn't make myself tell you at the time. Then the longer you don't say something, the harder it gets."

I know this from personal experience, having kept the loan I took out on Bella Flora to myself way longer than I should have. On the other hand, information is key. How can you prepare against things you don't know? And friendship should be based on honesty.

"Jeez," I say again but less emphatically. This is way too heavy a conversation for Christmas Eve. Sydney's revelation has knocked even the possibility of visions of dancing sugarplums right out of my head.

"I'm sorry for not telling you sooner," she murmurs. "I really am."

I'm exhausted and not remotely able to process this revelation or think about what happened five years ago. I'm not even sure why I'm so shocked that I wasn't his first choice when I already know I wasn't his last.

"I hope you'll forgive me, Ky."

"Mmm-hmmm." Despite the shock, my thoughts

are slowing. My eyelids get heavy. I begin to drift off.
I have way bigger issues with Daniel than the fact that
he came on to Sydney first all those years ago. I have
to reach a decision about the movie. I have to move out
of Bella Flora and turn it over to a stranger. I have to
be up in just a few hours. I try to push these things out
of my head, but as darkness descends this is exactly
what I dream about. Daniel and Sydney. Only it's now,
not then. Daniel and Sydney, whom he falls so madly
in love with that he actually leaves Tonja Kay and . . .

Something cold and wet touches my skin. There's a
snuffling sound attached. Visions of Daniel and Tonja
Kay and Sydney evaporate.

"Mommy?" A hand grasps my shoulder.

"Mommy!" It's Dustin. My eyes feel as if they're
glued shut, but Dustin needs me. I have to wake up. I
have to . . . "I need help!"

I don't know whether this is real or a dream, but I'm
a mother. I struggle out from under my covers and sit
up. I manage to swing my legs over the side of the bed
while trying desperately to wake up completely so that
I can take action. I can't seem to make my eyes open.
I don't understand what's happening. "What? What is
it? What's wrong?"

"It's my . . ."

My feet hit the floor. I start to rise. Which is when I realize that I'm standing in a puddle. A warm one. My eyes snap open.

". . . My puppy needs to go to the . . ."

We both look down at the yellow liquid I'm standing in.

Dustin looks up at me then back down at the puppy, who is apparently not quite finished.

"Oh no! Oh no you don't!" I scoop up the puppy and run for the back stairs, holding him out in front of me, careful not to slip in the droplets that jounce out of him as we descend. By the time we get outside he's finished and my feet aren't the only things that have been splattered.

I put him down on the grass and he sniffs around for a moment or two. He looks up at me. Then I swear he shrugs.

"Merry Christmas, Kyra! Can you and Dustin give us a smile, luv?" Nigel Bracken is wearing a red-and-green Hawaiian print shirt, no doubt in honor of the holiday. A red Santa hat sits at a jaunty angle on his head. He is not alone.

I look down at the ragged boxers and T-shirt I slept

in. I'm not wearing a bra or underwear and I am spattered with with puppy pee. I never want to see this picture or the caption they'll give it. But it's unlikely I'll be able to avoid it.

Dustin puts his hand in mine as the camera drives whir. He and the puppy look up at me. I'm pretty sure they're both smiling. "Is it time?" Dustin asks me hopefully. "Can we go in now and open presents?"

Chapter Six

Inside I notice everything I missed in our mad dash to get the puppy out to the backyard. Coffee is brewing. Conversations are taking place in the kitchen. Even my brother, who is always the last person to wake up on pretty much every occasion, has made it to the main house wearing something other than pajamas. Both he and Thomas Hightower, who are in the kitchen munching on coffee cake and cinnamon buns, look up and offer to go wake up Sydney.

I remind myself that it's Christmas, but the dregs of my nightmare are still with me and there's an internal clock I can't seem to turn off that's counting down the days until we have to turn our home over to some stranger.

"Go get dressed. Everybody will be here in an hour." My mother hands me a cup of coffee and points us toward the back stairs. "I put your favorite pants and sweater on your bed, Dustin. Do you want me to help you get dressed?"

"I kin do it." Dustin is already scooping the puppy up into his arms, and I am forced to accept that there's no way on earth I'm ever going to convince Dustin to give him back. He's barely let go of him since Santa delivered him. "We're going to have to figure out what to call him," I say as we tromp upstairs. "And we're definitely going to have to potty train him."

"Like me!" Dustin beams, still proud to have graduated to big-boy underwear.

"Right." Dustin pretty much trained himself, but I don't think dogs are motivated by the chance to wear Thomas the Tank Engine underwear. "We're going to have to make sure he understands that if he needs to go to the bathroom he has to do it outside."

He nods solemnly though neither of us have any real idea how to make this happen.

"If I get dressed real fast kin I jes open a little present?"

I give him the raised eyebrow Mom is so good at.

"Peeeassse. . . ."

I try the other eyebrow. "Everyone will be here soon to open presents."

"But I wanna . . ."

It's clear the eyebrow thing needs work, so I simply shake my head and turn my back. He's still protesting as I duck into the master bathroom to shower and dress since both my mom and Will are downstairs and Sydney has already commandeered the second bathroom. I'm done and heading back downstairs before Sydney shows herself, but then I didn't put on makeup or blow-dry my hair. Even back when I had no one to think about but myself, I wasn't thinking about those things.

My thoughts circle back to Daniel and I catch myself wondering just how diverse his taste in women really is. I mean, Sydney and I are friends but it's not because we resemble each other in any physical way. And neither of us looks remotely like Tonja Kay, which I guess is the point. *Ugh*. I do not want to spend Christmas morning thinking about Daniel, Tonja Kay, or any of the decisions I need to make. So I follow Dustin's voice to the kitchen where he's "helping" Geema and lobbying to open just one "teensy weensy" present and practically inhale a cinnamon roll and a glass of milk, hoping the sugar rush will put me in a more festive mood. Alas, it appears there's not enough sugar in the world, or at least in Bella Flora, to make my thoughts completely Christmas-worthy. I nonetheless work my way through two and a half cinnamon buns and a Christmas cookie trying, and am licking the sugar off my fingers when Sydney strolls into the kitchen in a clingy red dress looking as if she's been in hair and makeup.

It's a relief when the doorbell rings at nine o'clock sharp. Six or seven rings later the celebration kicks into high gear and Bella Flora is bulging at the seams. The Hardins and Giraldis are all here along with octogenarian Realtor and friend John Franklin, his wife, Renée, and her sister, Annelise, the original owners of the Sunshine Hotel. All twenty-three of us press into the salon, twenty-five if you count the twin babies that everyone takes a turn holding. I lift my video camera to my shoulder as the present-opening begins with Dustin's stocking and escalates into a gift giving and receiving free-for-all that is not for the faint of heart.

Everyone has brought a present for Dustin and by

the time he's done, a wall of gifts that's almost as tall as he is has risen around him. I can't help smiling at his pure unadulterated joy as I go in for a close-up.

"Is all for me, Mommy! Lookit what everybody gived me!" He buckles on the new tool belt from Avery and the Hardins, plucks the strings of the guitar that Will promises to teach him to play, and shrieks with excitement when Joe Giraldi wheels a shiny red bicycle complete with training wheels and a matching helmet out of the hall closet and helps Dustin on it.

"Thank you! Thank you!" He kisses cheeks and gives and receives high fives with a blissful smile that makes my heart swell. He's thrilled with everything, but there's no question which gift he prizes most. He doesn't let the puppy out of his sight and neither does Sherlock, though in Sherlock's case it's more about self-preservation and fending off the puppy's overly enthusiastic stealth attacks of affection.

Mouthwatering smells emanate from the ovens as the morning flies by to a soundtrack of Christmas songs and happy chatter. Just after noon, my father carves the turkey while Will slices the ham. I make sure to capture this on video because only my mother could have two men who love her working so close to each other with knives. Then we fill the water glasses while Avery and Chase, who are definitely flirting with each other, open bottles of wine. Bitsy tries to help, but it's clear she doesn't have a lot of experience in anything but being served. My mother, always the diplomat, assigns her to help Dustin fill baskets with rolls and biscuits and then carry them to the table.

Finally we sit down to a beautifully set table that positively groans with food. Mom sits closest to the kitchen so that she can jump up as needed and orchestrate the meal. I notice that she's glowing and capture it on video. There's nothing she likes better than feeding the people that she cares about. And pretty much all of those people are in this room right now. We join hands and bow our heads as she leads us in a simple nondenominational prayer of thanks. This is our village, the family we've chosen. I look from face to face then take in the room, the feel of this house that we know so intimately and love so much. Even if we have to vacate Bella Flora for a while to save it, *this* is our home. The place inside me that has been hollow with panic begins to fill. I reach for my wineglass and without further ceremony we chow down.

We're still eating when Dustin says he's had enough

and asks if he can go play with the puppy, who finally gave up on trying to convince Sherlock to play a while ago and is now curled up beneath Dustin's chair.

"Don't you think you should name him first?" I'm nursing a nice warm inner glow and I intend to do everything in my power to keep that glow going. "We have to call him something."

"We do," my mother says. "And it should be something special."

"Well, don't ask Nikki," Avery quips. "It took her an inordinate amount of time to name her children."

Nikki shoots her a look, but she doesn't argue. One of the twins did come home from the hospital without a name.

"How about Snarls Barkley?" My brother the basketball fan asks. "Or even Bark Obama in honor of our former president."

There's laughter.

"Or maybe Bark Wahlberg." This comes from the only one of us who resides in Hollywood and had a cameo on *Entourage*.

"Let's not overlook the music industry," Will says. "I kind of like Sinead O'Collar. Or Billie Howliday."

"Those are female singers," Thomas Hightower

points out. "We need a guy name." He grins. "How about Ozzy Pawsborne?"

"Or L.L. Drool J?" I throw out.

After that the suggestions come fast and furious.

"Jimmy Chew!" Bitsy throws in. "You know he'll be eating footwear. It might as well be designer."

"Bark Twain!" John Franklin goes for the literary.

"Sherlock Bones!" His wife Renée chimes in.

Sherlock lifts his head and snuffles while the rest of us laugh.

"We already hab a Cherlock!" Dustin says. I know most of this has to be going right over his head, but he's enjoying the spirit of the conversation as well as the laughter.

"If we're talking literature, I vote for J.K. Growling!" My mother, who loved the Harry Potter books as much as we did, says.

"Josh and Jason couldn't get enough of those books," Chase adds. "What do you think of Hairy Paw-ter?"

There's more laughter.

"I kind of like the sound of Droolius Caeser," Jeff Hardin adds.

"Anybody else like Anderson Pooper?" This comes from Joe Giraldi Sr.

We're really cracking ourselves up.

"Is there somebody you'd like to name him after?" I ask Dustin, thinking he might want to choose something that has to do with Christmas. I'm about to suggest Santa Paws when he looks at me and says, "Can I name him after Max Nemorah?"

"You want to name him Max Menorah?" I ask.

"Jes Max." For the longest time Max came out as "Gax." He stops and smiles an incredibly sweet smile. "I wanna name him Maaaax!"

There's a bit of a silence as those of us who knew and loved Max Golden blink back tears.

"I think that's a perfect name," my mother finally says, reaching for and squeezing Dustin's hand. "Absolutely perfect."

With that she directs the clearing of the table and all that is to follow. "Let's just carry things into the kitchen. We can have dessert outside once we refrigerate the leftovers. It's way too gorgeous to stay inside a minute longer than necessary."

• • •

Only Nigel and his cohort Bill are still skulking about as we move outside. If I had the slightest bit of sympathy for them, I'd offer a plate of food or a selection of desserts, but the warning about feeding strays goes double for paparazzi.

On chaises near the pool, Thomas and Andrew hang around Sydney like the Tarleton twins in the opening scenes of *Gone With the Wind*. She's polite, even friendly, but she's flirting on automatic pilot. I see her relief when they leave her alone to toss a football with the Hardins. There's talk of a flag football game down on the beach to make room for dessert, but nobody actually moves. If I could doze in a portable car seat like the Giraldi twins are or go back to bed right now, I would.

I've just plopped down on a newly vacated chaise when my cell phone rings. I let it go to voicemail because my entire family and everyone I care about are here right now. Do call centers operate on Christmas Day?

My eyes are getting really heavy when it rings again.

"I think you might want to answer this." My mother, who's passing by with a plate of Christmas cookies, picks up my phone and hands it to me. "Caller ID says Deranian."

I blow a bang out of my eye and wipe my free hand on the side of my jeans. Even with my mother watching

I'm tempted not to answer. I'm still irritated at Daniel's stunt last night. As cute as that puppy is, he shouldn't have given it to Dustin without asking me. With Daniel it's all about the drama, the grand gesture, without any thought about how the reality will play out for anyone else. I get up and carry the phone out to the seawall as I answer.

"It took you long enough."

I almost trip over my feet when I realize it's not Daniel, but his wife, Tonja Kay. "What do you want?"

I learned a long time ago that there's no point in attempting to be friendly. Tonja's never called for any reason other than to swear, threaten, or demand. I'm not in the mood for any of those things. I actually don't know where in Orlando they're spending the holiday. I've gone out of my way not to know. "I'm guessing you didn't just call to wish me a Merry Christmas."

"No."

I say nothing. She's the one who placed the call.

"I called to strongly encourage you to go ahead and officially commit Dustin to *The Exchange*."

Once again I leave the ball in her court.

"We'll make the experience comfortable for him. For both of you. You have my word on that."

I remain silent. I know just how much her word is worth. She'll go to the ends of the earth to make someone suffer for an insult or anything that smacks of betrayal, but make someone on her shit list feel good? I'm pretty sure that's not in her wheelhouse.

"I assume you've considered how upset Dustin will be when he's old enough to understand that you kept him from helping his father when he needed it most."

Tonja's mentioned this before. It's the only argument that carries weight. She's also made it clear that she'll be the one who will explain my dastardly deed and monumental selfishness to my son.

"This is not the day to discuss this. Not that there's anything to discuss, because I'm still thinking through my decision." I watch the wake from a Jet Ski splash the jetty. A speedboat moves closer. My focus is on the sound of gnashing teeth on the other end of the line.

"The only things you should be thinking about right now are your friends and family."

"What's that supposed to mean?"

"Oh, nothing in particular. But everybody's vulnerable, you know."

I absorb the threat even as I turn my back to the speedboat now idling off the seawall. Better an unflattering butt shot than a frightened look that Tonja might one day see. Daniel's wife is a predator. If she smells even a hint of fear she'll come in for the kill.

"You really are a piece of work aren't you?" I ask as if all I care about is getting back to dessert, which is currently being served on the loggia. "You don't care who you hurt or what you have to do to get what you want."

"I haven't noticed you worrying too much about others," she snaps. "Or you wouldn't have wagered and lost the house Daniel bought for Dustin."

I watch my brother fix a plate of dessert for Dustin and see Sydney pour him a cup of milk. Max wags his tail with excitement. I remind myself that this is real life playing out in front of me. The life she's trying so hard to muck up.

"I've had enough of this, Tonja. I realize you don't know me all that well, but the more you threaten me the harder it is for me to agree to anything," I explain as calmly as I can. This is the truth. I've listened to my gut way more often than I should. But I have absolutely no talent for acting. If I end up on that set with Dustin, I won't be able to simply suck it up and pretend that everything's okay. What will that do to Dustin?

"I'm not threatening, I'm promising," Tonja says in

a saccharine-sweet voice that is far more frightening than her curses. "You blow off this film and you and everybody you care about will pay the price."

We're already paying the price. A week from today Dustin and I are moving into a tiny Sunshine cottage with my mother so that a complete stranger can move into Bella Flora. "We really don't have anything left to discuss," I say. "I'll let Daniel know what I decide."

"The answer better be yes. And it better be soon," Tonja declares. "We need Dustin in Orlando on January fifteenth."

I have nothing to say to this. I'm aware of their plans and their timetable. I just don't want Dustin or me to be part of them. My stomach turns, and I know it's not the Christmas dinner that's to blame. I move toward Bella Flora in desperate need of the people who have spilled out of her. Everyone is scarfing up the desserts. Teams are forming for a game of flag football down on the beach. Captains Thomas and Andrew both try to draft Sydney.

Just before I disconnect the cursing begins. No one knows as many four-letter words as the angelic-faced Tonja Kay. No one. And I have the videotape of her shouting a lot of them to prove it.

Chapter Seven

Sydney, Thomas, and Andrew are in the salon watching football the next afternoon. My mother and Will have gone for a walk on the beach. I'm in the kitchen making a turkey sandwich for Dustin. My dad wanders in to get a beer, and I try once more to get information about Bella Flora's mystery tenant.

I had a dream early this morning just before Dustin and Max appeared at the side of my bed, that it was Daniel and Tonja who'd rented it simply to force me out. A couple of Christmases ago when she found out before we did that Daniel had bought Bella Flora, she threatened to gut her and put an indoor lap pool in the salon. She was not a happy camper when it turned out he'd bought it for Dustin and me. In my heart I believe that she'd drop a bomb on it if she could. Or take it apart brick by brick if she had the time. The only reason she mostly controlled herself on the phone yesterday is that she wants Dustin in the movie and has not yet achieved her goal.

"I'll make you a sandwich if you just tell me that it's not Tonja or Daniel?"

"I'd be glad to have the sandwich. But I actually don't know the name of the tenant. The rental was set up through a company that's owned by another company. I couldn't find anything about either of them online."

"Doesn't that seem like a lot of trouble to go to unless you're extremely wealthy or famous or both?"

"Well, anyone who could pay half a million up front and another quarter to exercise the second six month option has money. But it could be anybody who's looking for privacy. A corporate raider. A Mafioso. A . . ." He shrugged. "We don't know because they don't want us to. But I think it's safe to assume they aren't going to be holding keg parties or tearing the place apart."

"Why not? It could be some trust fund baby or

something." I pull out the ketchup and mayonnaise to make a Thousand Island dressing to smear on the bread.

"No offense to Bella Flora or the gorgeous ground she sits on," my dad says, helping himself to a handful of chips. "But someone young with that kind of disposable income isn't likely to choose this particular house in this particular location."

It's true that the population of St. Petersburg and St. Pete Beach, on which Pass-a-Grille sits, does tend to skew older than, say, the Panhandle or Daytona Beach or Key West. The standing joke is that if you leave a glass of water out someone will put their false teeth in it.

"You need to just accept this rental opportunity as the godsend it is. The money's sitting in escrow and will be transferred into your account at 12:01 A.M. January second." He pulls out a jar of pickles and a couple of paper plates. He's gotten a little handier in the kitchen since he moved into a place of his own. "If you want to reassure yourself, you can stop by and say hello after they move in."

This goes without saying. Wild horses couldn't drag me out of town until I make sure there is not a homicidal maniac or destroyer of property living in our home.

"You know John and I will keep an eye on everything." He puts down the half-eaten pickle. "Kyra, just do the film. Collect the rent. You'll be ahead of the game."

"Right." This sounds so much easier than it is. In fact, everything in my life sounds a hundred times easier than it feels. Just go spend six weeks on location with Dustin, Daniel, Tonja Kay, and family. Then just come back and live in a nine-hundred-square-foot two-bedroom cottage with your mother, son, and a Great Dane puppy for what could be a whole year while some rich stranger occupies the home you are forced to rent out. Oh, and don't forget to figure out how to salvage the career you thought you were building so that you can earn a living. I stop working on the sandwiches and try to slow the frantic beating of my heart. Because even if I somehow manage all that I'm still going to have to figure out what to say when Dustin gets old enough to ask why his "Dandiel" is married to someone else and has a whole other family.

I cringe at the whiny tone my thoughts have taken and am appalled at the panic that I feel. This is not the person I want to be, but it appears to be who I am. *Move on. Grow up.* The commands echo in my mind.

As the reverberation begins to fade, I try to grasp how such simple goals could seem so impossible to achieve.

. . .

"Oh my God! I can't believe this shit! There's no way that defensive end wasn't offside!"

I walk back into the salon a while later to see Sydney on her feet shouting at the television screen. Thomas and Andrew are on their feet, too. But they're looking at Sydney with admiration and a fair amount of lust. Dustin's eyes are glued to Sydney's face. They are wide with shock. Even Max looks surprised. It's not that I've never slipped and uttered a swear word, but it's always followed by a quick apology and explanation of all the reasons we shouldn't talk that way. You have to grab your teaching moments where you can. But Sydney is not apologizing or explaining. In fact, she looks like she'd like to charge the TV set and do the referee bodily damage.

"Maybe we need to step outside and cool off a bit." I take hold of Sydney's shoulders and aim her toward the French door.

"Me and Max wanna come, too!" Dustin and his shadow follow us out the door. Max makes it almost off the pool deck before he pees. I'm not sure whether to praise him for waiting until he was out of the house or pick him up and move him onto the grass so he knows where he's supposed to do his business. Dustin is already in the sandbox by the time Max finishes.

Sydney paces the pool deck, apparently still worked up about the bad call. I try to imagine getting that upset about a football play, but I just can't do it. I've already got too many things to worry about. Her phone rings. She answers gruffly then abruptly stops pacing.

As I watch, her face goes white. Her grip on the phone tightens. I see her take a deep breath, but she says nothing. I think maybe it's Jake. Or someone calling to tell her something she doesn't want to hear about Jake.

When she hangs up after not speaking a single word, she stares out over the water for a while before finally turning to me. Her face is pale. Her features are no longer animated.

"Was it Jake?"

She shakes her head.

"Are your parents okay?"

She nods. "As far as I know."

"Who was it?"

She looks at me as if trying to decide whether to answer. Finally she says, "Tonja Kay."

Now it's my turn to stare. "Tonja Kay called you?"

She nods again.

"What did she want?"

I'm not sure how Sydney manages to get the words through her lips given how tightly clenched her jaw appears. Actually all of her looks tightly clenched.

"She called to let me know that she has friends at the production company that produces *Murder 101*. That she knows I'm not pulling the audience I used to. And that they really need to consider making some serious casting changes."

She looks me right in the eye. "She told me that she knows someone who'd be way better in my part than I am. Someone who could take over if something happened to Cassie Everheart. You know, if they decided to write her—and me—out of the show."

"But Cassie Everheart *is* the show," I say. "And she has been from the beginning. You created her. You absolutely rock that part."

"Yeah, well. She reminded me that characters get killed off all the time. Then she pointed out that one quick call from her could change the trajectory of my career completely. You know?"

I know all right. That's exactly how I ended up off *Halfway Home* and out of the movie business. Tonja also threatened to take *Do Over* away from us, but in the end we managed to lose the show on our own. "Oh, God. I'm so sorry."

"I wanted to tell her to shove her threats up her ass, but that show . . ." She swallows. "That show is all I have."

We drop down on a chaise, our backs to the speed-boat still idling off the seawall. I am appalled by how much I hate Tonja Kay at the moment and how neatly she's boxed me in.

"She told me that if I convince you to bring Dustin to do the movie, she won't feel like she needs to make that phone call." She shakes her head. "But really I think the point is to remind you how much power she has and what she's capable of." She snorts inelegantly. "I'm just collateral damage. A lever she can pull that might get you to act."

I can barely swallow for the lump of anger and fear clogging my throat. That lump is wrapped in guilt. Whatever I do, somebody will get hurt. But you aren't supposed to give in to a terrorist's demands, right? Because then they know that their reprehensible acts work.

I keep my back to the photographers. My hands fist on my thighs. It takes every shred of self-control I have left not to cry or telegraph just how furious I am. "I am so, so sorry, Syd. I just . . . I promise I'll find a way to make things right."

"You just do what's right for you and Dustin," Sydney says. "I'm a big girl and there are other parts. Other shows." She gets up and walks slowly back into the house. She's not the same woman who was yelling her lungs out over a football game.

The truth is, there aren't unlimited roles floating around out there. Shows like *Murder 101* don't come along every day. And Tonja Kay has lots of pull in Hollywood and a vicious will to use it.

Chapter Eight

I drive Sydney to the airport the following morning, way too bummed to worry about disguises. The paparazzi know where we live, what we drive, and sometimes even where we're thinking of going. They're cunning in the way that wild animals are; in order to eat they must successfully stalk and fell their prey. They are the deer hunters in camouflage carrying powerful zoom lenses; we are Bambi.

We take the Howard Frankland Bridge over Tampa Bay, which is a bold vivid blue. The sky is filled with sunshine. My world is not. Threats I don't want to bow to and decisions I don't want to make are like dark clouds blocking the sun.

"You are not responsible for Tonja Kay's behavior," Sydney says as we take the airport exit. "You did not turn her into a bitch on wheels."

"No." I take a deep breath, but I can't seem to draw enough air into my lungs. "But I did put you in her crosshairs. And I am really and truly sorry."

"Stop apologizing," she tells me yet again when we arrive at Tampa International Airport. "We're survivors. Both of us. So we'll . . . survive."

People stop to stare at her as we hug good-bye. A lone photographer trails after her as she walks into the terminal. I hate that I'm the reason there's so little sway or spring in her step, that she's a beautiful but empty shell of herself. Spending the holiday with us left her facing even bigger problems than she had when she arrived. Dustin wasn't the only good thing that came out of my painfully brief time on the set of *Halfway Home*, and Sydney's friendship is not something I take lightly. Neither is her welfare. How can I possibly stand by and see the career she's fought so hard for trashed because of me? And what about Daniel?

My hands tighten on the steering wheel as I face a

few more harsh realities. Number one—however it sometimes feels, I am not Dustin's only parent. Number two—if I'm willing to accept gifts like the security of Bella Flora and Dustin's financial future, both of which *I* put at risk, doesn't Daniel deserve a say in his son's life?

By the time we get back to Bella Flora I feel as if I have my own personal dark cloud hanging over my head. Will and Thomas are getting ready to drive down to Mermaid Point. As we pull up in front of the low garden wall, I see my mother step into William Hightower's arms, and I'm reminded how fluky love and all the things that go along with it are. My mother found romance in her twenties and fifties. At the rate I'm going I'll be lucky if I ever date again.

Dustin hugs them both good-bye and then runs to me with his arms outstretched. I'll take unconditional and uncomplicated love over dating any day. Though I kind of hope it's not an either/or proposition.

Andrew's the next to depart. He's driving back to Atlanta and his job at Coke. I really can't get over the fact that he is now an employed adult. He lifts Dustin and whirls him around. There's a lot of chortling involved—not all of it's from Dustin.

"Take care of yourself, Ky." He hesitates. "You will let me know the next time Sydney's coming in, right?"

I look at him until he blushes then add an eye roll for good measure. I do not attempt the eyebrow lift.

"Hey, some women prefer younger men. You know, because we're at similar sexual peaks."

I seriously doubt that Sydney is one of them and, of course, she now has much bigger fish to fry, but given how deflated I feel I'm not about to pop anyone else's bubble. "Absolutely." I smile and then because no matter how tall or employed he is, he is my little brother, I wrap my arms around him and offer meaningless instructions. "Drive carefully. And text to let us know when you get home."

"That's exactly what Mom said." He grins.

"Well, she has taught me pretty much everything I know about parenting." I hug him one more time. "Come back soon. Even if Sydney doesn't."

Now Bella Flora is empty except for Dustin, my mom, and me, and I'm strangely reluctant to walk inside and feel that emptiness. Apparently I'm not the only one. We linger in the front garden watching Max sniff bush after bush, leaving his mark on the ones he likes best. We're still standing there watching him and looking slightly forlorn when a text dings in.

"It's Ray Flamingo," my mom says, brightening. "He's at the cottage and wants us to come look at a few things."

We're in the minivan and on our way before the image fades from the screen.

. . .

The Sunshine Hotel and Beach Club is a patchwork of midcentury buildings that we rescued from the bulldozer. It was built by Renée Franklin and Annelise's grandparents back in the early forties and operated as an American Plan hotel for mostly Jewish Midwesterners in the winter months and a summer beach club for locals until it closed in the eighties. Renée and Annelise's father died there under mysterious circumstances and Annelise's mother, a suspect at the time, disappeared. I shot and produced a documentary about the hotel's past and our restoration of it, which our former network has stopped me from selling. We all invested in the renovation—my contribution came from the loan I took out against Bella Flora. But we only had enough money to redo the main building, the pool area, and the grounds. The original one- and two-bedroom concrete cottages are just painted shells waiting to be finished out and customized by their owners.

Beach club memberships have been selling; the cottages haven't. Joe bought his and Nikki's two bedroom outright. Bitsy claimed hers in exchange for her sponsorship of the kinder, gentler version of *Do Over* we'd hoped to produce for ourselves, and Avery recently redid hers when she moved out of Chase's house. My mother and I are the last "investors" to claim one. If I can't find a way to hold onto Bella Flora, this could end up being our permanent home.

Our cottage sits about halfway between Avery and Bitsy's one bedrooms, not far from Nikki and Joe's two bedroom. A tall U-shaped hedge of trees and bushes that intertwined over the years wraps around the cottage area on three sides, hiding it from the street. The concrete path we're on now branches off to the main building, pool, and rooftop grille that overlook the beach and gulf.

The cottage area is small enough to put us all within shouting distance. We've been referring to it as Bestie Row since Avery moved in. Now there's no arguing with the name. If we could get a few more women we like to move in, we'd have a commune.

"Greetings." Ray Flamingo is his usual testament to sartorial splendor and is dressed in the pastel hues that he prefers. He's a gentle soul with a wicked sense of humor and a will of iron. And while he prefers to work with wealthy clients, the man knows a thing or two about how to stretch a dollar. He is extremely creative in the face of adversity.

Unable to save the original terrazzo floors, he's finished our concrete slab floor in a shiny white gloss and painted the walls and ceilings a soft white that makes the room feel larger. Rugs in abstract patterns of brilliant blues, citron, and shades of orange divide and liven up the space. A kitchen table under the window is flanked by two cushion-topped storage benches. Two bright tubular chairs that sit on either side of the window can be pulled up to the ends of the table or pushed over to the living area.

Ready-made bookcases have been joined together on either side of a small media console to create what looks like a custom built-in. The sofa is a sand-colored nubby chenille. Two small club chairs are covered in a bright paint-splattered canvas that's meant to be lived on.

I register these details and even add my admiration for how cleverly Ray and Avery have created additional storage, but my mind doesn't really want to absorb the fact that within a matter of days we're actually going to live here.

The hallway is lined with more storage in a patchwork of different-sized white cupboards and shelves. In the second bedroom a white tubular steel bunk bed has a full-size mattress on the bottom for me, and a twin with a railing around it on the top for Dustin.

My mother has the master bedroom with a bath that opens onto the walled garden. Dustin and I have the smaller, but perfectly serviceable bathroom—all of it fresh and clean with cheerful pops of color that should be lifting my mood but aren't.

I smile and tell Dustin how much fun it will be to "bunk" together, but in truth I'm trying not to hyperventilate. We have only a handful of days before we move in here. Which means I have only a handful of days left to decide whether we're going to do *The Exchange* or not.

I keep hoping there will be a mental "ding," kind of like an incoming text, and I'll simply know the right thing to do. But I'm running out of time to receive this revelation and my hesitation hasn't helped anyone, including me.

"The cottage looks really great," I tell Ray. "It's like something right out of a design magazine." I smile, but I can feel my lips quivering. Ray Flamingo is a good friend and an incredibly talented designer. But no matter what Avery builds in or Ray designs, nothing is going to turn this concrete cottage into Bella Flora.

· · ·

My dad picks up Dustin and Max for a sleepover the next afternoon. Well before the sun is set to go down, Nikki, Avery, and Bitsy arrive at Bella Flora to toast the sunset. Nikki whips up a couple pitchers of piña coladas, which we've decided are not only for summer anymore. Avery pours most of an industrial-size bag of Cheez Doodles into a bowl, and Bitsy arranges Ted Peters' smoked fish spread, which has replaced the pricier caviar she once dined on, on a plate, with the requisite hot sauce and crackers. Mom carries out a throw or blanket for everyone. After all, it is almost January and we are drinking frozen concoctions.

New Year's Eve is still a couple of days off, but this is the last sunset we're spending together before we have to vacate Bella Flora, so there's an unusual somberness to the proceedings.

Nikki reaches for her glass and stifles a yawn. "Gemma's teething and she was up all night. Every time I think I've got this parenting thing figured out something changes."

"Can we reframe that?" Mom asks.

"Okay . . . I was having trouble giving them both bottles when I was alone and I found this double harness/papoose thing that solved the problem. So, I have been licking things as they arise. Not as actively as Avery"—she nods to Avery who's been licking the Cheez Doodle residue from her fingers.

"Very funny," Avery says as everybody laughs. She now has cheese on her lips.

"The point is, I'm improving," Nikki says. "So, I guess figuring out how to adapt is my good thing. I mean, change can be good in its own right, right?"

"Yeah, well, in my world change isn't all it's cracked up to be." Bitsy pours us another round.

"So you're not enjoying your work at the law firm or here at The Sunshine?" Mom asks. "Isn't there some satisfaction in taking the hunt for Bertie into your own hands?"

"I do believe you're leading the witness, counselor," Avery interjects.

There's some laughter at that.

"All right, I'll go with taking charge of parts of my life that I used to leave to others," Bitsy says. "That does feel good. But it doesn't mean I'm not looking forward to having money again so I don't have to."

"Good thing accepted." My mother raises her glass and we all take a sip. "How about you Avery?"

"Well, I kind of feel like for every step I take forward I'm taking two back," Avery says, pushing her glass forward for a refill.

"But?" Nikki prompts.

"But, I did get a call from someone interested in a tiny house build. And dating Chase is kind of good."

We wait as she helps herself to another Cheez Doodle. Avery is not one to spill forth.

"He asked me out for New Year's Eve," she says finally. "And I guess there is something kind of exciting about starting fresh."

"That's not just good, that's great," my mother enthuses. She can insist all she wants that she's not the good enough police, but she totally is.

"And you?" I ask when I see her gaze begin to settle

on me. "Are you really okay with moving out of Bella Flora and having me and Dustin and Max living on top of you in the cottage?" I watch her face in the wash of rising moonlight. There's no question we will fill the cottage to the brim.

"Look," Mom says. "Having to move out of Bella Flora is painful. But we've been really lucky to live in her all this time. I mean, without Daniel she would have been in other hands a long time ago. At least this time it'll hopefully only be in other hands for six months to a year." Her eyes glow. Her positivity is stunning. "Besides, the cottage is cute and I'll never be sorry about living with you and Dustin. That's a plus in my book no matter the square footage. And I think your father has a date for New Year's Eve."

This *is* a good thing. My dad only recently stopped actively mooning after my mother.

"You really feel good about that?" Bitsy asks.

Mom nods. "The last couple of New Year's Eves my resolution has been to figure out what to do with my life. It'll be easier knowing that Steve is figuring out his own."

Her eyes fix on me again. But I really can't think of a single good thing that I can offer with any sincerity.

"Sorry," she says. "I know I have an overabundance of good things in my life right now. I didn't mean to run on like that."

I sigh. "Can't I borrow one of yours just this once? I mean, I *am* glad Dad is moving on. And we *are* lucky to be living with you. Even if we all have to imitate sardines in a can."

"Sorry, sweetie. But I think that would sort of defeat the purpose of the exercise. You need to come up with something good on your own."

There is silence around the table. I can almost feel Bella Flora pressing for an answer. I try not to listen because I think Bella Flora is also giving me some shit for handing her over to a total stranger.

"Maybe it would help if you tell us why you're having such a hard time coming up with something," my mom prompts.

"Seriously." Nikki jumps on the bandwagon. "You have a fabulous and healthy child. A single child. Who doesn't need diaper changing and who sleeps through the night. In my book that's like a slew of good things all wrapped up together."

"And you do have a roof over your head—it's going to be a smaller roof for a while, but you're not going to be out on the street," Bitsy says and I think about the Palladian Villa in Palm Beach that was stolen right out from under her.

"And you do have us," Avery points out. "In good times and in bad. In sickness and in . . ."

Nikki snorts and reaches for her drink. "We're close, not married."

"Tell us, Kyra," Mom says gently. "It's almost always better to share problems than to keep them bottled up inside."

"Fine." I draw a deep breath and force myself to meet their eyes. "Tonja threatened Sydney and her role on *Murder 101*." I take another breath even though the first one did nothing to calm me. "In fact, she's threatened everyone. If I don't let Dustin do the movie, she is going to rain shit down on all of us." I look at their faces and see the worry written all over them. The truth isn't setting anyone free. Although I wouldn't have thought it possible, I actually feel worse. "I can't tell you how sorry I am to have dragged you all into this."

The drink-or-despair reflex, a more modern relative of fight or flight, kicks in. We all reach for our piña coladas and take long, panicked gulps.

Nikki is the first to recover. "I'm not afraid of Tonja

Kay," she proclaims. "I have survived diaper rash, teething, and projectile vomiting that makes *The Exorcist* look like amateur hour!"

"I'm not afraid of her, either!" Avery says. "I watched Deirdre drop in front of me and I lived through Jason's teenage meltdown."

"Tonja Kay can go suck wind!" Bitsy says. "My husband stole everything I have and is having a baby with an exotic dancer. We've all been through a ton of awful and we're still standing."

"That's right." My mother stands and holds up her glass. "We are *strong*!"

"We are invincible!" Bitsy does the same.

Avery gets up and clinks her glass against theirs. "We are women!"

Nikki stands too and clinks glasses with all three of them. I'm afraid they're about to break into a chorus of "I am woman, hear me roar."

I stand because how can I not? We toast and drink and trash-talk Tonja Kay long past sunset. I apologize again for unleashing her fury on the people I care about most.

"Friends don't let other people abuse their friends!" Nikki drains the last dregs of her drink. "We reserve the right to do that ourselves."

Bitsy, who's the only one whose voice isn't the least bit slurred, laughs. But no one attempts to improve or correct Nikki's language. We all know exactly what she means.

The drinks and affirmations continue in the light of a rising moon. But their support doesn't make me any less responsible. All I've done is warn them and apologize. I do have the power to protect them; what I don't know is whether I have the nerve or the backbone required to do so.

Chapter Nine

I'm ashamed of the way I drag myself through, and ultimately waste, these last few days of the year.

I've always relied on my gut. Apparently when my gut fails me, I have no fallback and absolutely no talent for weighing and thinking. As any procrastinator knows, the longer you put something off, the harder it becomes. The pebble I began pushing up the hill months ago has grown into a Sisyphean-size boulder. I don't know how to budge it.

New Year's Eve is a quiet affair. Bitsy's visiting a former neighbor in Palm Beach. Avery is out with

Chase while my father is out with a woman none of us have met. Nikki and Joe are staying in with the babies. My mother could be at Mermaid Point with Will, but I think she's afraid to leave me alone in my misery.

I am well and truly ashamed of myself and my dithering. Mom handled much harder decisions and situations with poise, yet I seem to be wringing every agonizing moment out of this.

Mom, Dustin, and I spend the evening in pajamas. Because I promised Dustin he could stay up until the New Year, he conks out at his usual bedtime. I think I conk out not long after he does. Mom wakes me in plenty of time to watch the ball drop. Moonlight is glinting on the water when I take Max outside. Dustin's eyelids don't even flutter as I carry him upstairs and tuck the two of them in. My mother hovers in the doorway briefly and we look at each other. We both know this is not ideal, but we made it through exactly one night of trying to put them to sleep separately and given the packing and prepping we've been doing for the move, neither of us has the strength for it.

• • •

We watch the excitement in Times Square curled up in our pajamas on the salon couch and I'm pathetically grateful that I'm not alone. I sigh.

My mother brings her knees to her chest and looks at me. "So, have you made a decision?"

"Not quite."

Her eyes widen slightly. My mother is incredibly patient, but this is not a bible story and she is not Job.

"We move to the cottage tomorrow. We finish cleaning up Bella Flora tomorrow afternoon. After that it belongs to our tenant."

I nod, wishing I could deny it. There is no last-minute reprieve coming from the governor. The deadline has come. It should be a relief, but the ramifications of this decision hang over me like Damocles' sword. There is no win-win possibility, at least not as far as I'm concerned. If there were, I would have already chosen it.

"Kyra. This is it. Yes or no."

"I know," I say miserably. "I don't want him in that film. He's only four and I know how grueling it will be and how real that kidnapping scenario could feel."

Her eyes remain on my face.

"And I don't want to be on that set with him and Daniel and Tonja and their family." Well, at least I've finally come out and said it. My mother's look tells me this conversation isn't over, and that I don't get any points for admitting the obvious. "And I don't want the two of us to be in the center of the media storm. It's bad enough now when they show up to get an occasional shot or two. But that . . . that will be a category-five hurricane with an epic tidal surge."

She holds my eyes with hers. "Then don't do it. Say no. And live with the fallout. We're all prepared to do that if we have to. Just choose what's right for Dustin. That's all any of us want."

For some reason their understanding makes it harder, not easier. I am a mass of contradictions. None of them make sense.

"But just remember," she continues. "That even if he doesn't do this film, Dustin will always be Daniel's son. And you'll always be the woman who gave birth to his son out of wedlock. It might be better to learn how to handle it rather than hide from it." She's still looking me directly in the eye. "Better for both of you."

I want to jump up and leave the room. I want to end

this conversation and never have it again. But she does not drop her eyes or give me an inch of room to run. "So, I'll ask you once more. If you feel that strongly about avoiding the set and the attention, why haven't you already said no?"

I want to go outside and howl at the moon, which is now huge and high in the winter sky. My mother is still watching me. Waiting. In her quiet way she is as undeniable as the tides that moon controls.

"Because I'm afraid that Tonja is right, and that Dustin won't forgive me for not letting him help his father."

My mother's eyes probe as sharply as scalpels. I feel like I did when I was a child and told only half the truth. Will I ever know my son as well as she knows me?

"And?"

I swallow, but the truth can no longer be held back or denied. Not even from myself. "And although Daniel never really loved me as much as he pretended to, he does love Dustin that much. And he's been far more than generous to all of us." Her silence forces me to finish the admission. "It feels wrong not to help. I'm not sure I'd be able to forgive myself for not helping." I grimace. "I absolutely hate the idea of giving Tonja

what she wants. And I feel like I'm selling Dustin somehow to compensate for the mistakes I've made."

Mom sits back against the sofa. "I think you're con-
fusing the issues here, Kyra. Piling them all on top of
one another." Her smile is wry but gentle. "The money
is only a small part of it. I think you know that. Or you
will if you let go of all the side issues and focus on what
matters most."

I wait for her to tell me what to do, but she's watching my face. In the end all she says is, "You're Dustin's
mother. As a mother there's only one question you have
to answer."

"And that is?"

"What will be best for my child?"

I walk upstairs still uncertain. But when I crawl into
bed I feel the tension I've been carrying around for so
long begin to seep out of me. I lay my head on the pillow and sleep the sleep of the dead. No dreams. No
nightmares. Although it's not the incoming "ding" of an
arriving answer, something wakes me just before sun-
rise on New Year's Day.

I get up and go to the window to look out over the
grounds and across the water. I stretch. A while later
the scent of coffee reaches my nostrils, and I pad into

Dustin's room. Max opens one eye then burrows back underneath Dustin's chin. And I just know.

Quietly, I pull the bedroom door closed behind me and feel the weight I've been carrying evaporate. I've made my decision. It's one that I'm pretty sure I can live with.

Dustin and I are going to Orlando to do *The Exchange*. Not because of the money or the threats or for any other reason than because Daniel is Dustin's father. Period. Making Tonja's life better is just an unfortunate consequence.

I move to the back stairs, eager now to tell my mother.

Mom greets me as I enter the kitchen and one eyebrow goes up in a way I'm not sure I'll ever be able to emulate. I can see in her smile that she knows. "Good for you." She puts her arms around me and hugs me so tightly I can feel both our heartbeats. "I knew you'd figure it out. I'm sure they're up and eagerly awaiting your call."

"I don't know," I say as I step back. "I think I'm kind of hungry." In fact I can feel my appetite returning. And maybe even my sense of humor. "Let's have breakfast. Maybe we can make pancakes and sausage so we'll have strength for the move today."

"But I'm sure Daniel is waiting to . . ."

"I don't think I need to let them know right this minute, do you, Mom?" I feel a smile spread across my face.

If I'm going to give them what they want, I'm going to do it on my terms. Dustin can work for scale, not a million-dollar bribe. And I'll go along like any mother of a child actor might. But I won't lie. I kind of like the idea of making Tonja and Daniel sweat at least a little bit.

Mom pulls eggs and bread and milk out of the refrigerator while I pour myself a cup of coffee.

"So you'll call them after breakfast?" she asks as she begins to crack eggs into a bowl.

"Sure. Or maybe after lunch." I hear Dustin moving upstairs and a happy *woof* from Max. I feel so light I'm almost surprised my feet are still touching the ground. "Or I might call later this afternoon. You know, after the move." Oh, who am I kidding? I'm going to make them sweat as much as possible before I say yes. "Technically, I believe I have until midnight tonight to let them know."

BEST BEACH EVER

Available now from Berkley

Nicole Grant Giraldi stood in front of a far-too-full-length mirror that hung on a wall of the too-small cottage where she, her husband, special agent Joe Giraldi, and their twin daughters currently lived. It exposed two primary reasons women were not designed to give birth at forty-seven: lack of elasticity and surplus gravity. She closed one eye and shifted slightly, but the expanse of flesh did not become easier to contemplate.

Despite all of her fears and doubts, the body she was staring at had performed admirably. It had adapted and stretched to accommodate Sofia and Gemma. Against great odds, it had carried them full-term, propelled them into the world nine months ago, and then provided sustenance. What it had not done was snap back into anything that resembled its previous shape.

Her eyes slid away. She forced them back. It was time to accept reality. Her breasts hung lower than seemed anatomically possible. Blue veins streaked across them, no doubt to match the ones that now criss-crossed the legs she'd once been proud of. Stretch marks cut across the stomach that jiggled as she turned. Although she knew it was a mistake, she looked at her rear end, which had grown wider and had somehow been injected with cottage cheese. Most likely while she'd been sleeping. Or confined to bed rest.

"Are you ready?" Joe called.

She sighed and turned her back on the mirror as she wriggled into a jogging bra, slipped her arms into a T-shirt, and pulled the too-tight Lycra up over her thighs. "Almost!"

"I'm going to put the girls in the stroller. We'll be outside."

Nikki tied her hair back into a low ponytail, donned a lightweight running jacket, and laced up her shoes. Careful not to look at herself again, she left the bedroom and made it through the tiny cottage in a matter of seconds.

It was the second day of January. On the west coast of central Florida, that meant a vivid blue sky, butter yellow sun, and a cool salt breeze. She breathed in the crisp air as she stepped onto the concrete path that bisected the Sunshine Hotel property and nearly stumbled at the sight of Joe and the girls waiting for her.

Were they really all hers?

Tamping down a swell of emotion, she moved toward the stroller, taking in the pink and white knit hats tied neatly beneath their chins and the sunscreen slathered over their cheeks. Sofia had her father's dark hair, sparkling brown-black eyes, and sunny temperament, while Gemma was auburn-haired and green-eyed, like Nikki. Where Gemma's oversize lungs and the will to use them had come from was still under debate.

"All present, recently diapered, and accounted for. Requesting permission to move out." Joe shot her a wink and saluted smartly.

Though he was closing in on fifty, Joe remained broad shouldered and hard bodied with a chiseled face and piercing dark eyes that too often saw right through her—a skill she blamed on his FBI training. They'd met when he used her to help him catch her younger brother, Malcolm Dyer, whose three-hundred-million-dollar Ponzi scheme had left Nikki and then-strangers Madeline Singer and Avery Lawford with nothing but shared ownership of Bella Flora, a 1920s Mediterranean revival mansion at the south end of the beach.

She saluted back and fell into step beside him. A few doors down they passed the two-bedroom cottage that Madeline Singer, her daughter, Kyra, and her grandson, Dustin, had just moved into.

"It'll be great having Maddie here, but it's so strange to think of someone else living in Bella Flora," Nikki said, thinking of the house they'd brought back from the brink of ruin and that had done the same for them. After they'd first renovated Bella Flora, Dustin's famous father, mega-movie star Daniel Deranian, bought it for Dustin and Kyra. It had become home to all of them when they'd needed one most, but Kyra had been forced to rent it out.

"Yeah," Joe agreed as they wheeled passed Bitsy Baynard's one bedroom, which the former heiress had taken in lieu of repayment for the money she'd put into their now-defunct TV show. "When is Bitsy coming back?"

"I don't know. She said she was going to stay in Palm Beach until she found someone who knew something about where Bertie is hiding." Nikki grimaced. In her former life as an A-list matchmaker, Nikki had brought Bitsy, heiress to a timber fortune, and her husband together and had counted them as one of her biggest successes. Right up until last January, when Bertie disappeared with Bitsy's fortune and an exotic dancer who was pregnant with his child.

When the walkway split, they wheeled the stroller toward the low-slung main building, a mid-century gem they'd renovated for what they hoped would be a new season of their TV show, *Do Over*. The sound of voices and the scrape of furniture reached them from the new rooftop deck, where tables and chairs were being set up. The pool area was quiet. The lifeguard would take his place on the retro lifeguard stand at noon, when temperatures had risen and the rooftop grille started cranking out hot dogs and hamburgers.

By the time they wheeled through the opening in the low pink wall and onto the beach, Nikki was feeling slightly winded. Joe was not. Despite the weak morning sun and the breeze off the gulf, he pulled off his T-shirt and tucked one end into the waistband of his running shorts. His chest and abs were hard, his arms and legs muscled. Dark hair smattered with gray dusted his chest and arrowed downward. She considered his body with an unhealthy mixture of admiration and jealousy. And a devout wish that men carried the babies.

"You know we don't have to run," he said when they reached the hard packed sand near the water's edge. "It's a gorgeous day just to be outside."

"Definitely gorgeous," she agreed, admiring the dip and dance of sunlight on the slightly choppy water's surface. A wind surfer skimmed by as she began to stretch, his brightly colored sail bulging with wind. "But I know you're ready for a run." She had to hold onto his shoulder as she reached back to grab her foot and stretch her quads. "And so am I."

"All right." When she'd finished stretching, he flashed her a smile and opened his arms wide, leaving their direction up to her. "Lead the way."

To their right lay the historic Don CeSar Hotel and the northern half of St. Petersburg Beach. In the other direction . . . She shrugged as if it didn't matter, but she could not deny the tug she felt. Without a word, she pivoted left and broke into a slow jog, heading toward the southern tip of Pass-a-Grille. And Bella Flora.

Joe turned the stroller and fell in beside her. For a few heady minutes, she simply gave herself up to the fresh air, the wash of water on and off the sand, and the caw of gulls wheeling through the sky. But it wasn't long before her breathing grew uneven and her strides became shorter. She flushed with embarrassment when she realized that he had checked his stride to match hers. Her chin went up and she picked up her pace. She'd recently weaned the girls to formula, and while nursing had helped her drop weight, she was going to have to do more than a crawl if she ever hoped to get her body back. "You worry about yourself and the girls," she snapped, careful not to huff or puff. "I'll be fine."

"Okay," he said easily. "You're the boss." His movements remained fluid, but she could still feel him holding back. "There's no shame in taking it easy, Nik. And walking is exercise, too. A walk could be nice."

"Right." Surely that wasn't her breathing that sounded so . . . labored. Or her legs that had turned into lead weights. She pinned a smile on her lips and focused her eyes down the beach. She'd run this distance a thousand times. There was no reason she couldn't do it now. She *would* do it now. And if she felt a little uncomfortable, well, no one had ever died from discomfort. Otherwise, she would have expired early in her pregnancy. She picked up her pace another notch and ignored Joe's look of concern. She was not going to whine or complain, and she most definitely wasn't going to walk. Breathing was overrated. And it was nothing compared to pride.

• • •

Shortly before her life imploded, Madeline Singer had decided to refurbish it slightly. Her nest had emptied and she'd hit the big five-oh. The time seemed right to take down a few metaphorical walls. Raise a few ceilings. Open things up.

What she'd envisioned as a minor renovation turned into a total gut job when her husband lost everything in Malcolm Dyer's Ponzi scheme. The life she'd only planned to tweak got demo'd, blown to bits before her eyes.

There were casualties. Somehow, she managed to drag her family clear of the rubble. Ultimately, those who were still standing constructed a new life—one that bore almost no resemblance to the original. Not exactly a "do over," but a chance to do and be more.

Today was January second. The first usable day of a brand-new year, and once again, her life was under construction. Yesterday she, her daughter, Kyra, her four-year-old grandson, Dustin, and Dustin's new puppy, Max, had moved out of Bella Flora into the newly renovated two-bedroom cottage she stood in now. Soon, Kyra and Dustin would go to Orlando so Dustin could play his father's son in Daniel Deranian's directorial debut. At which point Maddie would be completely on her own. A fact that both excited and terrified her.

In the kitchen, the lack of counter space forced her to work more efficiently, and in less than fifteen minutes she'd assembled an egg soufflé, slid it into the oven, and set the timer. The soufflé was of the never-fail variety, guaranteed to pouf in exactly sixty minutes. Unlike life, which came with no guarantees and often "poufed" when you least expected it.

Soon the scent of melting cheese teased her nostrils and began to fill the air. She pictured it wafting down the short hallway to the second bedroom, slipping under the closed door, and crooking its finger. While she waited, she put on a pot of coffee and puttered, unpacking and organizing the exceedingly compact kitchen.

The cottage felt like a dollhouse after the castle-like Bella Flora, but Maddie felt oddly content. She lacked space and income, and her résumé consisted only of a brief and excruciatingly public stint on their renovation-turned-reality TV show. But the cottage belonged to her. And so did the new life that lay ahead.

A text dinged in and the face of William Hightower, the rock icon formerly known as William the Wild, appeared on the screen. A reminder that the life that lay ahead included a relationship with a man whose poster had once hung on her teenage bedroom wall.

Mornin' Maddie-fan. Hud and the fish send their regards.

Ha, she texted back. She had discovered early on that the fish that lived in the Florida Keys had a nasty sense of humor. Despite Will's efforts to teach her how to fly cast, she was no threat to the fish population, and they knew it. Catch anything yet?

Nope. But the sun's on the rise and it's so beautiful down here this morning I'm not sure I care.

Liar. Will loved to be out on the flats around Islamorada above all things, but he did not like to be bested by anything covered with scales.

True. And Hud's making me look bad. He and the
fish want to know when you're coming to visit.

They're just looking for entertainment. Hudson Power, Will's longtime friend and fishing guide, taught her to drive a boat and had been very patient with her ineptness at fly casting. But she was fairly certain she'd heard the fish laughing at her on more than one occasion.

True. He texted again. But I miss you madly, Maddie-fan.

A warm glow formed in her chest and radiated outward. She did not understand why Will, who had finally won his own personal war on drugs and was once again topping the charts, had chosen her when he could have his pick of younger, prettier, and undoubtedly firmer women, but she'd finally stopped asking. Plus, it was hard to argue with his physical reaction to her. Her cheeks flamed at the thought, and despite her two left thumbs, she was very glad they were texting and not FaceTiming.

When are you coming down to Mermaid Point? They had met when their former network sent Madeline, Kyra, Avery Lawford, and Nicole Grant down to the Keys with instructions to turn Will's private island into a bed-and-breakfast—an idea he did not appreciate in the least.

As soon as Kyra and Dustin leave for Orlando. Kyra, who'd met and fallen for the megastar on her very first film set, was not at all happy about the upcoming film. Or having to spend six weeks on set with Daniel and his equally famous movie star wife, Tonja Kay.

Can you tell me when?

In two weeks.

That's 2 weeks 2 long.

She was still smiling when she heard the first sounds of movement from the second bedroom. By the time she'd finished setting the dinette table, pulling the orange juice out of the refrigerator, and cutting up a bowl of fruit, there were only a few minutes left on the timer. A *woof* and the shake of a dog's collar were followed by the creak of a bed frame. Despite the early hour, the soufflé had worked its magic. She poured herself a cup of freshly brewed coffee.

Today was the first day of the rest of her life. Now all she had to do was figure out what to *do* with it.

· · ·

In the small second bedroom of her mother's cottage, Kyra woke to the scents of coffee and egg soufflé.

Dustin slept on the railed bunk bed above her. Max, the Great Dane puppy his father had unexpectedly and unaccountably given Dustin for Christmas, stood next to her bed, whimpering. She did not want to get up, but she also didn't want to clean up another accident.

Max nudged her with his wet, cold nose, and she threw off her sheets.

Today was not a good day. Today was the day a stranger would move into Bella Flora.

Max began to circle and sniff the floor. Kyra sat up, careful not to hit her head on the upper bunk. She was debating whether she could make a run to the bathroom when Max's whimper turned more urgent. "Got it. Hold on!" She grabbed him and raced for the door, holding him out in front of her.

"Good morning." Maddie moved to throw open the door.

"Um-hmmm." She sniffed appreciatively as they passed the oven that held the soufflé. Madeline Singer was the mother everyone deserved but didn't necessarily get. She'd created a home everywhere they'd landed, from the initially uninhabitable Bella Flora, to Max Golden's neglected Deco home on South Beach, to the rickety houseboat tethered to William Hightower's dock.

While Max anointed the grass and the nearest bush, she lifted her cell phone and roused it. The first six months rent had been released from escrow and deposited into her account, but the sight of all those zeros didn't make her anywhere near as happy as it should have. It meant there was not going to be a last-minute reprieve. The tenant would move in today. For the next six months, he/she/they would have the run of Bella Flora and the option to stay on for six more months after that.

Which meant she and Dustin and Max could be sharing a bedroom in Maddie's cottage for an entire year while a stranger lived in the house they'd poured their hearts and souls into and that was "home" in every way that mattered. She'd been a fool to believe that everything would somehow magically work out when she'd taken the loan to finance the Sunshine Hotel renovation and their own version of *Do Over*.

Max woofed happily as she pulled a plastic bag from her pocket, picked up his offering, and then dropped it in a nearby trash can. She'd changed Dustin's diapers easily enough, but she'd known the day would come when he could use the toilet on his own. Unless they moved into a rural setting, Max was never going to be able to dispose of his own droppings. She did not want to think about how big Max was going to get, or what size plastic bag he would one day require.

Inside, she found Dustin sitting at the dinette, drinking a cup of orange juice and chatting with his favorite person. That person held out a cup of coffee.

"Thanks, Mom." She swallowed a long sip, let the warmth slide down her throat. "The money's in my account."

"That's a good thing, Kyra. That will definitely take some of the pressure off."

"I know. But . . ."

"Come eat." Three plates containing soufflé, buttered toast, and fresh fruit were on their way to the table. Within seconds, Kyra was seated. She picked up her fork, but her appetite fled almost immediately.

"Kyra, you need to let go of the worry. It's done. Bella Flora's only on loan. She still belongs to Dustin and you. Emotionally, she'll always belong to all of us."

"It's just . . ." Kyra took a bite of soufflé, but her usual bliss over the cheesy wonderfulness was missing. She needed to see the tenant for herself. Needed to make sure he wasn't some Attila the Hun of houses, bent on destruction. Or someone fronting for Daniel Deranian and Tonja Kay for some nefarious reason she'd yet to figure out. She took another bite of soufflé and washed it down with another long pull of coffee.

John Franklin was meeting the tenant at eleven to hand over the key. She stole a glance at her phone. It was early. There would be plenty of time after a leisurely breakfast to shower and dress and discover that she'd left something at Bella Flora that they couldn't possibly be expected to live without.

• • •

Avery Lawford did not want to get out of bed. Not now. Not ever. She clutched the pillow more tightly to her chest and kept her eyes shut. It would take a crowbar to pry them open. A tow truck to move her.

Something warm passed under her nose. It smelled

dark and steamy before it moved just out of range and then back again. The lovely fog of sleep that had enveloped her began to dissipate. She closed her eyes tighter and wished she could shut her nostrils, but Avery braked for coffee. She drank it for the protection of others and had the T-shirt to prove it. She burrowed deeper into the cocoon of blankets, but her nose betrayed her.

No. She would not be ruled by coffee. She was stronger than coffee. The smell retreated. She'd begun to relax back into sleep when the crinkle of paper sounded near her ear. There was movement. A new scent joined the first. She sniffed—a reflex, nothing more. She was only human. *Sugar.*

"Avery?" Chase Hardin's voice was warm and seductive.

"There's nothing you could say or do that would make me get out of this bed right now."

"Nothing?" The bed dipped as he sat on its edge. "You mean you don't want this Dunkin' Donuts coffee or these glazed donuts?" He waved each item as he mentioned it. His voice grew muffled as he took a bite of donut and chewed appreciatively. "Ummm, that's good." He bent over and kissed her with warm lips sticky with sugar. This was what came of sleeping with a man who knew your weaknesses.

She opened her eyes. A large Styrofoam cup of coffee sat on the nightstand.

Chase finished off the donut, licked his fingers, and grinned. "I don't remember the last time I spent almost two days in bed." His blue eyes glittered. Dark stubble covered his cheeks, and his hair stuck up in a variety of directions. "I thought we needed sustenance." When she didn't make a move, he drew a donut out of the bag and placed it on a napkin next to the cup of coffee.

She'd known Chase since childhood, much of which she'd spent crushing on him. They grew up on their fathers' construction sites, went their separate ways. She became an architect. He took over Hardin Morgan Construction. He'd been a royal pain in the ass the whole time he was helping them renovate Bella Flora. And then one day he wasn't.

"Your cupboards are bare," he said. "A man cannot live on sex and Cheez Doodles alone."

"This woman can," she replied, stung that he would disparage the snack that, in the darkest of times, could help make life worth living.

"I give that donut and coffee about fifteen seconds." He looked at her knowingly.

She wanted to argue. And she really, really wanted to be asleep. She could resist if she wanted to. She could. But what would be gained by rejecting a warm, gooey, glazed donut and a steaming cup of coffee?

"If you were looking at me like you're looking at that donut right now, we could spend another two days in bed." He stretched and scratched his chest. "I owe my sister big time for having Dad and the boys up for the week." His blue eyes turned dark and steamy. They were a magnetic force. The siren call of coffee and donuts grew softer as a shiver of anticipation snaked up her spine. They'd been in bed since New Year's Eve, and today was . . . "Oh, no!" She sat up.

"What?"

"What day is it?" She ran her hands under the covers, but her phone wasn't there.

"It's Monday."

"Are you sure?"

He nodded without hesitation.

"But that means it's . . ."

". . . January second," they said simultaneously. But

it was just a date on the calendar to him. She began scooting out of bed.

"What time is it?"

He glanced down at his watch. "It's . . . ten forty."

She took one bite of donut, swallowed it whole, and grabbed the cup of coffee. "How far away did you park?" She moved toward the bathroom, very glad the cottage was so tiny.

"Hmmm?"

"You didn't park here at the Sunshine, right? I told you I didn't want anyone to know that we're . . . you know . . ." She nodded toward the bed, which looked like it had been struck by a hurricane. Or lifted by a tornado and tossed around for a night or two.

"Everybody knows, Avery. There's no reason to keep it a secret that we're back together."

"But we're not back together." She raced into the bathroom, turned on the shower, darted back to retrieve the donut. "Having sex doesn't mean we're back together. It just means we're still attracted to each other and spent a couple of days in bed to celebrate the New Year."

Their relationship had foundered during his youngest son Jason's meltdown and rebellion. Jason was doing better now and repeating his senior year of high school, but Avery could still remember exactly how it felt to be pushed away when things got rough. Other than Maddie, Nikki, and Kyra, the Hardins were the closest thing to family she had, and yet Chase had completely shut her out when Jason had gone off the rails. Out of the family and out of Hardin Morgan Construction.

That they were dating again was due to his abject apologies and powers of persuasion. She enjoyed his company, and the sex was spectacular, but she didn't intend to open herself up to that kind of hurt again anytime this millennium. And she was not prepared to tie her career to his.

She devoured the donut in a few hungry bites, and then stepped into the hot shower. Ten minutes later, she was running a comb through her short, blond hair and pulling on a pair of jeans and a *Do Over* T-shirt. She could almost hear her mother's ghost hovering above her and sighing over her lack of makeup, but she was a wash-and-wear kind of girl. And though she no longer hid the Dolly Parton bust that was too large for her height in oversized clothes, she had not yet reconciled to the big, blue eyes and Kewpie doll features that caused strangers to deduct IQ points before she even opened her mouth. "Are you staying here or coming with me?"

"Where are we going?" He grabbed the bag of donuts.

"Out."

"Out where?"

She grabbed the keys to the Mini Cooper and headed for the front door.

• • •

Nikki and Joe sat at their favorite picnic table at the Paradise Grille overlooking the white sand beach and the gulf that it bound. A stream of beachgoers passed in both directions. A jovial game of corn hole played out in the soft sand nearby.

Sofia and Gemma snoozed happily in the stroller, their faces smeared with the remnants of a scrambled egg breakfast. Seagulls eyed the crumbs left on their plates, but so far no dive-bombing had occurred.

"God, they're adorable when they're asleep," Nikki said, looking at the girls' angelic faces. "Not that they aren't adorable when they're awake, but . . ."

". . . You're too busy trying to keep them happy to notice."

Nikki looked at Joe. "You don't even bat an eyelash when Gemma goes on a screaming jag. Or one of them projectile vomits all over you."

"I may have ended up in the financial crimes unit, but I do have hostage negotiation training," he said wryly. "I know how to look like I'm not panicking, even when I'm scared shitless."

"So when do you think you'll be able to actually start negotiating with them?"

"Well, we know from personal experience that it doesn't work on pregnant women," he said. "I can't remember convincing you of a single thing while you were carrying them. So, while I don't know that there's a lower age limit, it's clear that rational thought is necessary. And probably the ability to speak, or at least understand and process language."

"Great." Nikki slumped. Every morning she vowed this would be the day that she'd become competent and unharried. The kind of mother who loved her children so much that she never resented the endless demands that created the near-constant state of exhaustion.

"I've got another ten days or so, and then I'm going to have to start traveling again."

Her heart sunk further. "Oh?"

"Yeah. Which is why I really think we ought to hire someone to help you."

"No. I'm their mother. Taking care of them is my job." Not a job she'd ever imagined for herself. But it wasn't one you could resign from.

"Nik, they're too much for the two of us a lot of the time. I can't leave you alone."

"I won't be alone," she said, trying to keep the panic out of her eyes and her voice. "Maddie will help. And . . . Avery and Bitsy will be nearby." Neither of them mentioned that Bitsy had fallen down on the job the night Nikki had gone into labor.

"Kyra and Dustin will be leaving for Orlando in two weeks. And Maddie won't have a reason to stay here. She'll be free to travel. Or spend time with Will. Or whatever she feels like. And Avery and Bitsy have no experience with children and aren't looking to acquire it. Plus, they'll both be working."

"I can do it," she said. "End of conversation."

"But Nikki, I . . ." His face smoothed out. She saw him relax his features, his shoulders. Hostage negotiation training her ass. "Ready to head back?"

She'd barely made it this far. In fact, about halfway

there, she'd been doing more of a brisk walk than a slow jog.

"I was thinking maybe I could run back to the cottage and come pick you all up in the car." He looked at her face. "You know, in case you'd like to just chill here for a while."

"Don't think I can make it back?" she challenged, though she wasn't totally sure she could. She only knew she was not going to appear too tired or too overwhelmed or too anything in front of him.

"No, of course not. I just thought you might want to get back more quickly. It's getting close to eleven."

"Eleven?" She sat up.

"Yes."

"I wouldn't mind walking a little farther. There's really no rush to get back, is there?"

"No."

"The girls love the jetty. And the fishermen on the dock."

He gave her a long look. "Sure. Why not?" He busied himself gathering the paper plates and cups and was gentlemanly enough not to say anything when she took her time getting to her feet.

• • •

"That was one of your best egg soufflés ever, Mom. Right, Dustin?" Freshly showered and dressed, Kyra strode back into the living room/kitchen, where Dustin stood on a stool, "helping" his grandmother wash the dishes.

"D'licious," he agreed, waving his hands, which were encased in a pair of too-large rubber gloves. Max was under the table, licking up the bits of egg that surrounded Dustin's chair.

"What do we say to Grandma?" Kyra asked Dustin as she stole a glance at the clock on the wall, and then turned her gaze to the coffee table, where the car keys typically ended up.

"Thank you, Geema!" Dustin crowed.

"You're both very welcome," Maddie said, hiding her smile at the speed with which Kyra located and pocketed the car keys.

"If you don't mind keeping an eye on Dustin, I . . . I have a couple of things I need to take care of." Kyra didn't quite meet her eye as she laid a kiss on Dustin's head and moved toward the door.

"Things?" Maddie asked.

"Umm-hmmm."

"Dustin wanna do things, too!" Dustin clambered down from the step and held out his arms. Maddie peeled the large, yellow gloves from beneath his armpits and down his arms.

Kyra checked the clock again.

"It's ten fifty," Maddie said. "Where exactly are you going?"

"Oh, you know. Here and there. Not far," Kyra babbled. "I won't be gone long."

"Kyra . . ."

Her daughter looked up, as if she'd been caught with her hand in the cookie jar.

"I really don't think this is a good idea."

"I . . . don't know what you're talking about," Kyra protested.

"It would be better to just stay away," Maddie said gently.

"Stay away from what?" Kyra adopted an expression of surprised confusion, but any mother worth her salt could read a daughter's face like a road map. It would take more than feigned indignation to make Maddie believe she was headed out to run errands.

"Kyra."

"Fine." Kyra sighed. "It's not like there's any chance of keeping a secret when we're living on top of each other like this, anyway."

"If you're going, we're going with you." She picked up the leash and attached it to Max's collar, and then handed Dustin his sweatshirt.

"Where we going, Geema?" Dustin asked as his mother pulled open the cottage door.

"If I'm not mistaken, I think we're going to Bella Flora, to get a look at the person who's going to live there."

Kyra breathed deeply as she drove south on the narrow two-lane road, but each breath carried its own little dart of panic and fear of who and what she'd find at Bella Flora. She turned on to Gulf Way, her thoughts jumbled and her gaze slightly unfocused. The familiar scenery rippled and shimmered before her eyes, giving the mom-and-pop hotels and expensive new homes on her left a fun-house vibe.

The blocks were short, and the avenues that stretched from the bay to the gulf were even shorter. At the Hurricane Restaurant, her foot eased off the gas pedal so the minivan passed Eighth Avenue, Pass-a-Grille's "main street," at what could only be called a crawl. The closer they got to Bella Flora, the slower she drove, and the sharper and more pointed the panic became. *What if the tenant is Daniel Deranian or Tonja Kay, or one of their emissaries? What if they're trust fund babies with no respect for other people's property? What if they look unstable or have a herd of children who abuse Dustin's mini Bella Flora playhouse?* The number of things the new tenant would be free to do to her home bombarded her. How could she let some stranger sleep in her bed? Hang their clothes in her closet? Lie on their couch? Mix drinks in the Casbah Lounge? *How on earth did I let this happen?*

"We can still turn around. It's not too late." Maddie hesitated. "No one will ever know we even thought about doing this."

Though she was driving as slowly as a new retiree, Bella Flora's gravitational pull was simply too strong to resist. So was Kyra's urge to protect her, even though it was far too late for that.

They passed a couple pushing a jogging stroller. That couple was Nikki and Joe. So much for a lack of witnesses.

And then she came face-to-face with Bella Flora,

rising out of the low, walled garden. A pale pink wedding cake of a house with banks of windows framed in white icing trim and bell towers that topped a multi-angled, barrel-tiled roof and jutted up into the brilliant blue sky.

"We going home?" Dustin asked uncertainly.

God, she wished they were only coming home from a trip to the grocery store or some other mundane errand and not about to watch some stranger move in. Eyes blurred with tears, Kyra pulled into a parking space. The blue Mini Cooper in the next spot belonged to Avery Lawford.

Max gave a happy *woof* as they joined Avery and Chase on the sidewalk. A minute later, Nikki and Joe arrived, the twins sound asleep in the stroller. Kyra was trying to decide who looked the most embarrassed when a lone figure walked up the path from the jetty. Gatsby-style pants fluttering lightly in the breeze and a mint-green vest buttoned over an oxford shirt, Ray Flamingo, former designer to the stars, walked up to them. "Beautiful day, isn't it?"

"Don't even try to pretend you were just out for a stroll," Avery said.

"Who, me?" Hands in his pockets, Ray turned to

face Bella Flora. "I didn't realize a house could send a distress signal until today."

"You know that whoever is renting Bella Flora has spent a lot of money to live in her," Joe said gently. "We have every reason to expect that person will treat her well."

John Franklin's Cadillac pulled up in front of Bella Flora at exactly eleven A.M. The car was a classic, like its octogenarian owner and driver. Kyra's father, Steve, who now worked at Franklin Realty and had been responsible for finding Bella Flora's mystery tenant, was with him.

With Max straining against his leash, Kyra and the others trundled over to meet them.

"You all look a little more like a lynch mob than a welcoming committee." John Franklin had a tuft of white hair around an otherwise-bald scalp and a long face dominated by the droopy, brown eyes of a basset hound. Those eyes looked worried as his hands tightened on the handle of his cane. "Is there a problem?"

"That depends," Kyra said.

"On what?" her father asked.

"On whether the tenants look as if they can fully appreciate their luck in getting to walk through Bella

Flora's front doors. If they don't, I might need help stringing them up from the Reclinata Palm out back."

Chase and Joe laughed. Maddie, Avery, and Nikki exchanged worried glances.

"We don't necessarily have to deliver a welcome basket," Ray said in a conciliatory tone. "But I don't think we need to be contemplating violence, either."

"Neither do I," Maddie said. "In fact, I'm not altogether sure we should be here." As usual, Kyra's mother seemed intent on keeping the peace. And preventing Kyra from committing a stupid act. If only that had happened before Kyra took the loan out against Bella Flora. "But clearly we're all curious to see who's moving in. So I think we should at least *act* like a welcoming committee. Plus, we can let them know we're nearby if they have any questions about the workings of the house."

They milled relatively quietly until a car turned off Pass-a-Grille Way onto Beach Road, passed the Cottage Inn, and pulled into Bella Flora's brick driveway. The car was low, sleek, and silver, with tinted windows that revealed little.

They inched closer, stopping just short of the garden wall as John and Kyra's father walked up the driveway. Kyra wasn't the only one holding her breath as the driver got out of the car. Through the palms and tall bushes, she could see only slices at a time: a lone male head of blond hair, a body that seemed tall and well formed. There was a flash of blue jean and some kind of dark jacket or blazer. He moved with a confident stride that Kyra chalked up to arrogance. Did that mean he would be careless with other people's possessions? Or did it mean that he was used to nice things and would take care of theirs?

She moved to get a better look, but everyone was jockeying for position. Between the bushes and trees, John and Steve's backs were the only things clearly visible. Steve froze briefly. John Franklin's normally hunched shoulders went stiff. Murmurs of what sounded like surprise reached them.

Heart pounding, knees pressed against the concrete, she leaned over the garden wall. The tenant cocked his head, and she sensed him peering between John and her father, as if looking for something or someone. Kyra felt Dustin let go of her hand as he moved toward the driveway. A prickle of unease raised the hair on the back of her neck, but she knew from the blond head and build that it wasn't Daniel Deranian. Was it another movie star? A famous athlete or musician?

"Lookit Mommy! Lookit who's here!" Dustin shouted as he ran up the driveway.

Kyra detached herself from the wall and the group to race after him. The breath caught in her throat as the tenant stepped around the two realtors and reached down to pick up Dustin. She blinked rapidly, trying to make sense of what she was seeing.